BLOODSPORT

A squad of steel-capped, leather-jerkined strangers had invaded his parents' clearing. At their feet lay his mother, her head nearly severed from her twisted body.

All his control shattered. He heard the soldiers' shouts of fear, saw the terror in their eyes as he leaped into their midst. For a moment, he had the advantage as they milled about and tripped over each other. But there were too many of them, and all were seasoned warriors. Before he could inflict any more damage, the club was sliced from his hands and a sword point bared three of his ribs.

Wounded, weaponless, the tery ran. And he would have escaped easily had not the captain thought to order his men to their mounts.

"Don't run him through!" he heard the captain yell. "Just keep slicing at him!"

It was great sport. He was a bloody ruin by the time he collapsed.

Laughing, they left him for the scavengers. But he didn't die.

The tery remembered that captain's face.

F. PAUL WILSON

THE TERY

BAEN
BOOKS

THE TERY

Copyright © 1990 by F. Paul Wilson

Portions of this novel have appeared as: "He Shall Be
John" in Fiction #4 in 1973 and "The Tery" in Binary
Stars #2 in 1978.

"Pard" is copyright © 1972 by Conde Nast Publications.

A Baen Books Original

Baen Publishing Enterprises
260 Fifth Avenue
New York, N.Y. 10001

ISBN: 0-671-69855-9

Cover art by Larry Elmore

First printing, January 1990

Distributed by
SIMON & SCHUSTER
1230 Avenue of the Americas
New York, N.Y. 10020

Printed in the United States of America

CONTENTS

THE TERY

PROLOGUE

It had become a subvocal litany—

> *A whole planetful of Christians*
> *Too good to be true*
> *Bound to be disappointed*

         —running through his head in a reverberating circuit until all other thoughts and considerations were blurred to indistinction. But the defeatism inherent in the phrases could not dampen the anticipation that grew tingling throughout his body as he approached the chapel.

The planet had been opened only recently to outside contact and trade. Its original settlers had cut themselves off from the rest of humanity many centuries ago. But their descendants—most of them, anyway—had different ideas.

The present population was divided into two nations. The smaller island country—inhabited, it

3

was said, by "Talents," or something like that—
wanted nothing to do with the Fed and so were to
be left quite alone. The larger nation, however, wel-
comed the chance to rejoin the mainstream of
inter-stellar humanity, and it was in this segment
of the population that Gebi Pirella, S.J., was
interested.

His mission was one of critical importance to the
Amalgamated Church of Unified Christendom because the inhabitants here had been described as
followers of a distinctly Christian-like religion, complete with crucifixes and all. It had been mentioned by earlier trade envoys who had been
permitted a brief glance inside one of the chapels
that the crucifixes were somehow *different*, but no
specifics were mentioned.

No matter. News of the existence of a planet-
wide Christian enclave would prove to be incalcu-
lably important to the stagnating Unified Church,
spreading its name and hopefully drawing converts
from all over Occupied Space.

"The cross is just a symbol, of course," Mantha
was saying as he pointed to the top of the chapel.
He was a big, fairhaired man wearing only a loin-
cloth in the heat. His grammar and speech pattern
carried an archaic ring. "Not an object of worship.
We revere the one who died upon it and hold to
the lesson of brotherhood he taught us."

"Of course," Father Pirella replied with a con-
curring nod.

Not only was that heartening to know, but it
was the largest piece of religious information he
had been able to pull from this taciturn native who

seemed to serve as some sort of ecclesiastical administrator to the locale.

The Jesuit had pushed their initial conversation toward a discussion of theological concepts but soon discovered that he and Mantha did not share the same vocabulary on religious matters. Beyond determining that the religious sect in question was less than two centuries old—unsettling, that, but surely not without a satisfactory explanation—his most basic questions had been met with an uncomprehending stare. He had suggested that the easiest and most logical solution was to go to the nearest structure and start there with concrete articles. After establishing a little common ground, they could then progress to abstractions.

Mantha had agreed.

The native held the door open for him—hinges . . . the technological level here was startlingly depressed—and Father Pirella entered the cool dim interior.

There was no altar. Stark and alone, a huge, life-size crucifix dominated the far end of the chamber. He hurried forward, eager to study it. Merely to find the Christ figure here on this isolated world would be quite enough; but to demonstrate that it held a central position in the culture would be more than anyone in the order or the Church had ever dreamed. It would be the consummation of—

"Mother of God!"

The words echoed rapidly, briefly in the dimness. Father Pirella's feet began to slide on the polished floor as he recoiled in horror at the sight of the figure on the cross. Crushing disappointment fanned his indignation.

is sacrilege!" he hissed through clenched framed in tight, bloodless lips. *"Blasphemy!"*

For a moment he almost gave in to the urge to hurl himself at the astonished and totally confused Mantha, then he shuddered and rushed out into the bright, wholesome daylight.

"I did not know what you were looking for," Mantha said when he finally caught up to Father Pirella, "but I had a feeling you would not find it in there."

"Why didn't you warn me?"

Mantha gently took the priest's arm and began to lead him down a path through the trees.

"Come. Come with me to God's-Touch and you will perhaps understand things better."

Father Pirella allowed himself to be led. God's-Touch? What was that? It certainly couldn't be any worse than what he had just seen.

"Everything starts a long time ago," Mantha was saying. "One hundred and sixty-seven of our years, to be exact. It begins in a field not too far from here . . ."

I

They hadn't left him for dead. They had to know he was still alive, had to see the shallow expansion and contraction of his blood-smeared rib cage as he lay on his face in the grass. But there were other stops to make and he took such a long time dying. A tery didn't merit a final stroke to end it all, so they left him to the scavengers.

Consciousness ebbed and flowed, and every time he opened his eyes it seemed that the world was filled with flies and gnats. He found he was unable to lift his arms to brush them away. Each time he tried, the effort involved dropped him into oblivion again. Which wasn't a bad place to be. Dark and quiet, there was no pain there.

But he always came back. Soon, if he was lucky, he would remain sunken there forever. Why not stay there? Everyone who meant anything to him had been taken away.

The creak of a poorly lubricated wooden axle

pulled him up to consciousness again. He heard
stealthy footsteps through the ground against his
left ear and allowed himself to hope.

Maybe another tery . . .

Summoning whatever reserve was left in his
body, he pushed against the ground with his right
arm and tried to roll over. The daylight suddenly
dimmed and he knew he was losing consciousness,
but he held on and managed to get a little lever-
age from his left arm, which had been pinned
under him. He moved. A shift in his shoulder
girdle and suddenly he was rolling onto his back
amid a cloud of angry flies.

The effort cost him another period of awareness.
When he came to again, the creaking was gone.
Despair crushed him. The furtiveness of the footsteps he had heard was proof enough that they
belonged to another tery, for stealth simply was
not the way of the human soldiers who trampled
everything in their path. Now the footsteps were
gone and with them his last hope of rescue.

He was dying and knew it. If the hot, drying
sun and his festering wounds didn't kill him by
nightfall, one of the large nocturnal predators would
finish the task. He couldn't decide which he—

Footsteps again!

The same ones, light and stealthy, but much
closer now. The passing creature must have seen
some movement in the tall grass as he rolled and
come over to investigate. He had probably crouched
at a cautious distance and watched.

The tery lay still and hoped. He could do no
more.

The footsteps stopped by his head and suddenly

there was a face looking down at him—a human face, bearded, with bright blue eyes. He lost all hope then. If he could have found his voice he would have screamed in anguish, frustration, and despair.

But the human neither ignored him nor further mistreated him. Instead, he squatted beside him and inspected the near countless lacerations that covered his body. His face grew dark with . . . could it be anger? The tery was not adept at reading human expressions. The man muttered something unintelligible as his inspection progressed.

Shaking his head, the humam rose to his feet and moved around to a position behind the tery's head. He bent down and hooked a hand under each of the tery's arms and tried to lift him. It didn't work. The human lacked sufficient strength to move his considerable weight, and the slight change in position he caused sent a white hot jolt of pain through each of his countless wounds. The tery wanted to scream to him to stop, but all he could manage was a low, agonized moan.

The human loosened his grip and stood up, apparently uncertain of his next step.

"Can you speak?" the man asked.

The tery was startled by the odd question. Yes, he could speak. He tried but his tongue was too thick and dry and swollen for a single word.

"Can you understand?"

The tery closed his eyes. Why the questions? What did it matter, anyway. He was going to die here. Why didn't this strange human just go away and leave him in peace?

After a short pause, the man tore a strip of cloth

from the coarse shirt he wore and laid it over the tery's eyes. Then he strolled away. The sound of his retreating footsteps was soon joined by the creak of the wooden axle. Both eventually faded beyond perception.

It was a small act of kindness, that strip of cloth, and totally incomprehensible to the tery. Why a human should want to keep the flies off his eyes while the rest of him died was beyond him, but the comfort it afforded was appreciated.

The sun blazed on him and he felt his tongue grow thicker and drier during the periods of consciousness which seemed to be growing progressively shorter. Soon, one of those periods would be his last.

He was brought to again by minute vibrations in the ground at the back of his head. Trotting hooves, and something dragging. The soldiers were returning. He was almost glad. Perhaps they would trample him as they passed and end it all quickly.

But the hoofbeats stopped and footsteps approached —many feet. The cloth was pulled from his eyes with an abrupt motion and the faces that leaned over him were human but didn't belong to soldiers. There were four of them and they glanced at each other and nodded silently. One with blond hair turned and moved from view while the others, much to the tery's surprise, bent over him and began to brush the flies and gnats from his wounds. All this without a single word.

The blond man returned with one of the mounts. From a harness around its neck, a long pole ran along each shaggy flank to end on the ground well beyond the hindquarters. Rope was basket-woven between the poles.

Still no word was spoken.

Their silence puzzled him, for they were obviously on their guard. What was there to fear in these woods besides Kitru's troops? And what had these humans to fear from Kitru, who slew only teries?

Further speculation was delayed by the appearance of a water jug. Its mouth was placed against his lips and a few drops allowed to trickle out. The tery tried to gulp but succeeded only in aspirating a few drops, which started him coughing. The jug was withdrawn, but at least his tongue no longer felt like dried leather.

With the utmost gentleness and an uncanny coordination of effort, the four men lifted the tery. The pain came again, but not as bad as when the first one had tried to lift him. They carried him and placed him across the webbing of the drag, then tied him down with cloth strips. All without speaking.

Perhaps they were outlaws. But even so, the tery began to think them overly cautious in their silence. The soldiers were long gone.

The humans mounted and ambled their steeds toward the deep forest. The uneven ground jostled the drag and caused a few of his barely clotted wounds to reopen, but the tery bore the pain in silence. He felt safe and secure, as if everything were going to be all right. And he hadn't the vaguest notion why he should feel that way.

The path they traveled was unknown to the tery, who had spent most of his life in the forest. They passed through dank grottos of huge, foul-hued fungi that grew together at their tops and

nearly blocked out the sun completely, and skirted
masses of writhing green tendrils all too willing to
pull any hapless creature within reach toward a
gaping central maw. After what seemed to be an
interminable length of time, the group passed
through a particularly dense thicket and came upon
a clearing and a camp.

The tents were crude, all odd shapes and sizes,
and scattered here and there in no particular ar-
rangement. The inhabitants, too, offered little uni-
formity of design, ranging from frail to obese. This
was hardly what the tery had expected. He had
envisioned a pack of lean and wolfish outlaws—
they would have to be feral sorts to hold their own
against Kitru's seasoned troops. But there were
women and children here and a number of them
took leave of their working and playing to stare at
him as he passed. These people hardly looked like
outlaws.

And the silence was oppressive.

His four rescuers stopped and untied the drag
from the mount, then lowered it gently until the
tery was lying flat against the ground. One of them
called out the first and only word spoken during
the entire episode.

"Adriel!"

A girl with reddish blond hair emerged from a
nearby hut. She was young—seventeen summers,
perhaps—slightly plump but not unpretty. Seeing
the tery, she rushed over and dropped to his side.
Gently, she examined his wounds.

"He's cut up so bad!" she said. Her voice was
high and clear and full of sympathy. "How'd it
happen?"

"Those are sword wounds," one of the other men said with some impatience. "That can only mean Kitru's men."

"Why'd you bring him back?"

The first man shrugged. "It was Tlad's idea."

"Tlad's?" There was a note of disbelief in her voice.

"Yes. He found the beast earlier and somehow convinced your father that we should help it. So your father sent us after it."

Adriel's brow furrowed. "Tlad did that? That doesn't sound like him."

The man shrugged again. "Who can figure Tlad anyway?" He indicated the hut. "Your father inside?"

"No." Adriel rose and pointed to a far corner of the camp. "He's over there somewhere, talking to Dennel, I think."

The men left in silence. The tery watched the girl duck back inside the hut.

Tlad? Was that the name of the man who had spoken to him and placed the cloth over his eyes? *Tlad.* He would have to remember that man.

Adriel soon reemerged with a wet rag and knelt beside him.

"Oh, you poor thing."

He was riding the ragged edge of consciousness then, and the last thing he remembered as everything faded into blackness was the cool, wet cloth wiping the dirt and dried blood from his face and a soft voice cooing.

"Poor thing . . . poor thing . . ."

II

"Think he'll live?" someone said behind her.

The sound of a voice startled Adriel. She gave a small cry and turned. A bearded man, tall and muscular, stood there, peering over her shoulder.

"Oh. Tlad. You startled me. You shouldn't sneak up on people like that!"

"Sorry. How's he doing?"

"I think he'll pull through. If his wounds don't fester too much, he should be all right."

"Good." Tlad gave her a quick nod, then he turned and started to walk away.

"Wait. I don't understand."

He looked back, his eyes flicking over her.

"What is there to understand?"

"Why did you bring my father news of a wounded tery?" she asked. "Why convince him to bring it in?"

"He needed help and I couldn't manage him. I figured you'd like the job."

14

"Oh, you did, did you?" She resented this relative stranger's presumption in assuming that he knew what she'd like.

"Yes. You both look like you could use a friend. You'll be good for each other."

Adriel stared into his unreadable face. The insight at the heart of his casual statement was so on-target that she was momentarily speechless. She looked at him closely. His light brown hair hung lankly against the darker brown of his beard. He was dirty and he smelled bad and she had never much liked him. He returned her stare.

"That was nice of you," she said, finally.

"Forget it. You and he are running from the same thing—I thought you might want to help him out a little. And he looked like he needed all the help he could get. Do a good job."

"I don't need you to tell me that!" she said sharply, letting her annoyance at his remark show. *Of course* she would take good care of the tortured beast!

He barked a short laugh and strolled to his wagon. With a single, smooth motion, he bent, grasped the two handles, and started off into the woods, trailing the wagon behind him. A few shards of broken pottery rattled in the back; the left wheel squeaked on its axle.

She watched until the thicket swallowed him up, then returned to her work with a scowl. Tlad had risen in her estimation today by his show of compassion for the poor beast unconscious before her, but she still did not like him. She couldn't pin it down, but there was something about that man that caused her to mistrust him.

Still, in a way she wished he had stayed longer. At least he was someone to talk to.

She went back into the hut to get some clean rags to bind the tery's deeper wounds, and when she returned, she saw her father approaching across the clearing.

"That thing still alive?" he said when he reached her side and stood surveying the bulk of the tery.

Komak was a man huge in height, girth, and spirit. His shaggy red hair and beard encircled his head like a mane; his skin was the type that never seemed to tan—it was always red from exposure to the sun despite the fact that he spent all of his time outdoors these days; and his eyes were a clear, pale blue. Adriel shared his coloring in hair, skin, and eyes, but was shorter and had a smaller frame.

"Of course he's still alive! And I'll keep him that way!"

Didn't anyone have any confidence in her?

Komak lifted the unconscious creature's upper lip to expose its sharp teeth.

"So this is Tlad's tery. Ugly brute."

"He's not so bad. He's just all cut up and his fur's all matted with dried blood. He'll look a lot better when I've had a chance to clean him up."

"Now that we've got him, what're we going to do with him?"

"I want him as a pet, father. And don't you ever call him 'Tlad's tery' again," she said with mock severity. "He's mine now."

"I don't know about that. Look at the size of him—the muscles in those arms. If he should ever turn on you . . ."

"He won't," she said assuredly. "He knows I'm his friend. I could see it in the way he looked at me when I started washing off his wounds."

"Well, we'll see."

"Father," she said after a pause while she tied a knot in the bandage, "are Kitru's men hunting and exterminating the forest teries, too?"

She remembered how all the teries in and around the town had been killed or driven off by the Overlord's decree. That had been awful, but at least the soldiers had not gone hunting through the forests for them. That had changed now, it seemed.

Komak squatted beside her. "Yes, I'm afraid they are. Overlord Mekk's new decree applies not only to us but to the forest teries and even to some of the more bizarre plants—at least that's what Rab told us."

"And where is this Rab fellow everybody talks about?"

"I don't know." He let his body slip back and rested on his buttocks. "But I wish he'd get here."

With a slow, almost painful motion, he lay back on the ground and closed his eyes.

"Tired?" Adriel asked, stopping her ministrations to the tery and looking at her father with concern.

"Exhausted. I'm not cut out for this. I didn't want to be leader of the group. When I agreed to the position, I thought it was only for a few days . . . until Rab showed up. Now it's been months."

"Where could he be? Do you think he got caught?"

"Possibly. When he warned us, he said we didn't

have much time to get away from the keep. Maybe he tarried too long trying to make sure everybody got out."

Adriel remembered the day vividly. Her father had hurried home from Kitru's court where he had long served as an advisor on matters of design and construction around the keep. He was in a state of great agitation. An unknown Talent who called himself Rab had whispered to his mind about secrets in old books and about a messenger on his way from Overlord Mekk with a new proclamation —an addition to the old Tery Extermination Decree. It ordered all the local lords to hunt down and slay all teries everywhere. But that was not what had so upset Rab and all the Talents—it was the second part, which included possessors of the Talent as offenders against God. Possessors of the Talent would thereafter be declared teries and summarily condemned to death without trial.

Word spread rapidly among those with the Talent—Rab, whoever he was, had contacted many of them—and the majority believed him. The Overlord had long been under the spell of a fanatical religious sect which worshipped the True Shape. All deviations from True Shape were considered unholy. Apparently the sect's dogma now excluded possessors of the Talent from True Shape.

There had been doubters among the Talents, of course. Those who claimed that it went against all existing laws to order their deaths merely because they possessed the Talent. These few stayed behind while Komak, Adriel, and the others packed whatever they could and fled into the woods. If they were wrong in trusting Rab, Komak had told them, all it would cost them was a few days of inconvenience and perhaps a little embarrassment. If they were right . . .

The wisdom of their choice became horrifyingly evident on their third night in the woods when the anguish, pain, and terror of the other Talents left behind in the keep leaped through the darkness to wake them from their sleep. The agonized emotions winked out bit by bit as those trusting Talents were systematically captured in their homes and dragged to the burning pit outside town. Only Adriel had slept on, oblivious to it all.

"I still say it's not fair to call us teries!" she said. "We're not! We're people!"

He smiled at her sadly. "My poor little Adriel. I indulged you and spoiled you, and now I've had to tear you away from all the luxuries I worked so hard to give you. I'd give anything to make things right for you again."

Adriel fought the tears. She missed her house, her clothes, her room, her bed, her friends, the shops, the marketplace in the square, *people who talked!*

Her father sighed and changed the subject. "I don't think Rab is coming."

"Maybe Rab is right here in this camp and we don't know it," she told him, hoping to buoy his spirits.

Komak opened his eyes and raised himself up on one elbow. "Not possible. I don't know how to explain it to you but . . . but once you've communicated with someone via the Talent, you'll always recognize him again. Rab isn't here."

"Maybe he's Tlad, then. We don't know anything about him."

"But Tlad doesn't have the Talent. You said so yourself. And you should know—you're the Finder."

Yes, she was the Finder, all right. Sometimes she wished she weren't.

"Still," she said, "there's something about that man I don't like, don't trust."

"Don't trust? He's never harmed you or any of us. As a matter of fact, he's been a good friend to us."

"Perhaps 'don't trust' isn't exactly what I mean. I don't know. He's sneaky. He always seems to be watching us. Maybe he's working for Kitru, spying on us."

"If that was his plan, my dear, he could have led the troops here long ago. And don't forget how he acted on behalf of the tery here—no man of Kitru's would do that."

But Adriel would not allow her suspicions to be put to rest. "I can't explain what he did today, but—"

"Don't try to explain Tlad," her father cut in. "He's not like us. He lives alone out here, makes his pottery, and doesn't bother anyone. Doesn't seem to be much afraid of anyone, either. But forget about him now. We have more pressing matters at hand."

"Oh?" She finished up the last dressing on the tery and looked at him.

"Yes. It's rumored that Overlord Mekk is planning a personal inspection of all the districts soon and that's probably why Kitru is sending his men out into the bush to kill off the teries: He wants to make a good impression on the Overlord." He paused for a moment, then: "This creature was found much too near the camp for comfort. Kitru's men might stumble on us next. We must move on. And soon."

Adriel watched him rise to his feet and stand with hands on hips, letting his eyes rove the oppressively silent camp. All motion ceased abruptly as everyone turned to face her father. After a short pause, he turned back to her. The camp dissolved into a flurry of activity.

"As soon as you finish with him, start gathering your things. We move at daybreak tomorrow."

III

They numbered near fifty, these strange, silent folk. As the predawn glow lightened the western sky, the tery watched their wordless coordination in fascination. They broke camp with incredible swiftness, loaded their pack animals, and prepared to start off through the forest toward a new and safer location.

Still weak from his wounds, the tery found himself beset by blurred vision and nausea every time he tried to raise himself to an upright position. He had passed the night in a deep, exhausted, untroubled sleep to awaken alert and chilled in the dawn.

Adriel, however, was up before him and ready.

"There, now," she said softly, pressing his shoulders back against the drag on which he had spent the night. "You don't have to go anywhere and you shouldn't." Her voice was soft and reassuring, its tone meant to convey the meaning of the words she didn't know he could understand. "See if you like this."

She placed a shallow earthen bowl filled with milk and bits of raw meat before him. With two or three brisk movements, he shoveled all the meat into his mouth, swallowed convulsively, then drained the milk.

Adriel's mouth hung open.

"You must be famished! But that's all for now—you'll get sick if I let you eat as much as you want." She poured some cool water into the empty bowl. "Drink this and that'll be all until later."

When they were all set to go, the tery's drag was bound again to one of the mounts. Adriel covered him with a blanket and walked beside him, a reassuring hand on his shoulder, as they began to move.

The tery considered his benefactress. She had a clear, open face in which he could read little. She appeared neither happy nor unhappy, neither contented nor frustrated. Lonely, perhaps? He thought that for the daughter of a chief—at least her father *seemed* to be the chief—to be lonely was unusual. Perhaps she wasn't pretty by human standards.

As they moved through the trees, a young man came up and matched his step to hers. He was well built with curly brown hair and an easy smile. A wispy attempt at a beard mottled his cheeks.

"How's the Finder today?" he said.

She sighed. "How do you think, Dennel?"

"Same old problem?"

Adriel nodded.

"Won't you ever understand?" he asked with a grin. "Speech is such a burden for us: thoughts flash as entities between us, whole concepts transfer from one to another as a unit, in an instant! We converse in colors and emotions and mixtures I can't even begin to describe! We don't leave you out on purpose. It's just . . . well, why walk when you can fly?"

"I know all that, Dennel. We've been over this before, but it doesn't help. It doesn't keep me from feeling left out. Back at the keep I could at least go and find some regular folks to talk to. But here . . . here I'm the only one who was born without the Talent."

"But the Talent came out in you in a different way! You're a Finder!"

"I can *find* possessors of the Talent, sure! But I can't communicate with them. I'm cut off!"

"But your ability to find makes you the most valuable member of the group. Through you we can find new members to add to our ranks. And we need every Talent we can find." He glanced up and down the column of travelers. "Every single one."

"That still doesn't keep me from feeling like a cripple," she replied sulkily. "And I'm still just as much a tery as you are, according to Overlord Mekk. So he wants to kill me, too. I get all the danger but none of the benefits!"

In the silence that followed, the tery had time to ponder what he had just heard. He now understood why these humans were fleeing Kitru. They, like the teries, were now on Mekk's extermination list. Humans had always enjoyed killing each other, his mother had told him. This was just another excuse to do more of it. His mother also had spoken of these people once: they were called Talents, or *psi-people*. That explained the eerie silence of the camp—they spoke with their minds. All except Adriel.

"Teries!" Dennel said, his eyes flashing. "This whole situation is so *foolish!* We're not teries! Everyone knows that teries are a product of the Great Sickness—dumb, misshapen animals, like this brute here."

"And you think you're not?" said another voice.

Adriel and Dennel reacted with surprise, but the tery had heard his approach. His heart warmed at the sight of the human who had caused his rescue yesterday.

"Oh, hello, Tlad," said Dennel. "And yes, I'm sure our special talents didn't come from the Great Sickness."

"How do you explain them, then?" Tlad's eyes danced. He seemed to enjoy challenging Dennel's conceits.

"Talents are a *refinement* of humanity, an *advancement*. I should think that is quite obvious. We can do things no one else can do."

"That doesn't necessarily make you popular with the rest of us who have to communicate by noisier means."

"Nevertheless, we should be courted rather than persecuted. We're the next step up the ladder."

"Maybe so," Adriel said softly. "But maybe Mekk doesn't like the idea of being left on a lower rung."

"By the way, how's the tery?" Tlad asked casually.

Adriel immediately brightened.

"Coming along, poor thing. He heals fast. Some of his smaller cuts are almost closed up already."

"Thanks to you, I'm sure," Tlad said, then waved. "I'm going ahead to find your father."

Dennel watched Tlad leave. "I'm not sure I like the way he comes and goes. He always seems to know where we are."

"Lucky for the tery that he knew where we were yesterday," Adriel said.

Dennel leaned over to get a better look at the wounds, then quickly turned away.

"What's wrong?" she asked.

"Just thinking: That could be you or I some day if the troopers ever catch up with us."

"But they won't," Adriel told him, her optimism bright and genuine. "My father can keep us one step ahead of Kitru's men without even trying. But let's not worry about it—it's too early in the day for that."

"All right," he laughed, and looked at the tery again, this time from a greater distance. "At least he's not a talker and not *too* ugly. Looks like a cross between a big monkey and some wiry breed of bear."

The tery disliked Dennel's tone but had to agree with the comparison. He was about the height of a man when he walked upright, although he much preferred to go on all fours. His hands were large, twice the size of a man's, and he was covered from head to toe with coarse black fur which was short and curly everywhere except the genital area, where it grew long and straight.

"Talker?" Adriel said, glancing between Dennel and the tery.

"Sure. Some teries can be taught to speak, you know. I saw one with a traveling music troupe that

came through the keep a few years ago. Some of
them sang, some of them danced, and one even
gave dramatic readings of poetry. But that was
before Mekk declared them 'unholy.' "

"Really? Do you think maybe I could teach this
one to talk?"

Dennel shook his head. "I doubt it. First of all,
I've been told that you've got to start them young
if you're going to have any success. And secondly,
you have to be lucky and get one who can be
taught. The degree of intelligence varies greatly
from one to another."

"Oh," she said with obvious disappointment. "I
thought I might have someone to talk to."

"They can't *think*, Adriel. At the very most, all
they can do is mimic sounds. And I'm not so sure
you'd want a talker around anyway. Some of them
are so good you'd actually think they had a mind."

"I guess it would be a little frightening at that,"
Adriel admitted.

The tery could have destroyed Dennel's misin-
formed theories in an instant, for he was a "talker"
and had no doubts about his ability to think. But
he kept to himself. If these humans found the
thought of a talking tery repugnant, how would
they feel if they knew that this animal was listening in on their conversation and understanding
every word? He needed them now—especially
now—while he was wounded, alone, and helpless.
He couldn't risk alienating them, so he remained
silent.

"By the way," Adriel asked, "just what does the
word 'tery' mean?"

Dennel shrugged. "I haven't the faintest idea.

As far as I know, they've always been called teries.
The name probably originated during the Great
Sickness."

Dennel excused himself and walked toward the
front of the train. As the tery scrutinized the psi-
folk around him, he began to understand Adriel's
predicament. Glances would pass between individuals, someone would smile, another would laugh,
but speech was used only on the pack animals to
keep them moving.

Adriel was indeed a lonely girl.

When the train halted at dusk, the tery was
finally freed from the drag and allowed to take a
few painful steps. At first his joints were stiff, his
muscles tight and inelastic, but gradually they loosened up. He walked in slow circles. It was good to
be up and about again. His spirits rose, but not
too far.

When he stopped moving, he noticed that only
two of the larger wounds had started bleeding
again, and those very little. Adriel had done an
excellent job of cleaning and binding the wounds;
his animal vitality would do the rest.

She appeared carrying two bowls. The sight of
her smiling face warmed him.

"Hungry?" she asked as he limped toward her.

He had been given small amounts of milk during the day and now there was another portion of
raw meat in the second bowl. He ate slowly this
time, savoring the flavor. It was the flesh of a fleet
grazing animal called *ma*. They were extremely
hard to catch and it occurred to him that there
must be some good hunters among the psi-folk.

Adriel murmured soothingly and examined each one of his bandages as he ate.

"Looks like you're coming along fine. You'll be back to your old self in no time." She sobered suddenly. "Then I suppose you'll take off into the bush again. You don't have to go, you know. We'll treat you well here, really we will. You'll have food and shelter and a friend: me."

The tery considered this.

Later, well fed and freshly bandaged, he followed Adriel to the community dining area but remained at a respectful distance, accepting the occasional table scraps the psi-folk offered him, almost enjoying the game of playing a dumb animal.

The progress of the meal, however, was an awe-inspiring sight: Bowls were passed in all directions, crisscrossing the table in dizzying patterns, hands reached and were filled, portions were dispensed into goblets and onto plates in precisely the desired amounts—all without a single word. Only Adriel's tiny voice and an occasional belch broke the silence at odd intervals.

When bellies were full, and the tables and pottery cleaned and cleared away, the group gathered around the central fire for what appeared to be some sort of conference. Adriel hung back, looking indecisive, unaccountably hesitant. Finally, after two or three deep breaths, she strode forward to where her father sat in silence. The big man smiled as she knelt beside him. The tery remained in the background at the perimeter of the firelight, watching, listening.

"We were just discussing the future," her father

told her, "and it looks as if we'll be spending years
in these forests." Suddenly he glanced sharply at
Dennel, whose face flickered on the far side of the
flames.

In Komak's eyes, the tery could almost read his
message to the younger man: *Haven't I asked you
to use your tongue when my daughter is present?
If not out of kindness, then at least out of courtesy!*

Grudgingly, Dennel spoke. "But you haven't
given my idea due consideration, Komak. We could
make ourselves very useful to Kitru—and to Overlord Mekk himself. Think of the intelligence net-
work we could form for him. Why, he could know
what was going on in any one of his provinces at
any time!"

"Spies for the Overlord?" someone shouted.
"Never!"

"Listen to me!" Dennel said. "It could save us,
and be beneficial to Mekk as well!"

"You're dreaming," Komak said. "Practically can't
touch Mekk these days. He's become a religious
fanatic. The priests have poisoned him against anything that does not bear True Shape—and that
now seems to include our minds. No, Mekk is
unreachable, I'm afraid."

"What about Kitru?" Dennel said. "We could
make him a very powerful lord."

Komak shook his head. "Kitru fears Mekk and
dares not disobey him. I should know after spending years as his advisor. Kitru is a cruel, venal,
greedy man, hungry for power, but he's a coward
where Mekk is concerned. He won't question a
single aspect of the new extermination decree. In

fact, he'll enforce it with a singlemindedness as fanatical as Mekk's, just to impress the Overlord."

"But we could be *useful!*" Dennel insisted.

"You mean 'used,' don't you?"

"No. We're humans! Citizens! We shouldn't be treated like teries! There has to be a way!"

"A man is only what he proves himself to be," Komak said with an abrupt note of finality. "Right now we're fleeing for our lives, but your alternative strikes me as worse. Should we prove ourselves to be slaves? Tools of a tyrant? I think not, even if he permitted us to live that long. We can only run for now, but Rab promised that someday we'd return—and on our own terms!"

"Rab!" Dennel said derisively. "The mystery Talent!"

"But where is Rab?" Adriel said. "The answer means more to me than the rest of you. Most of you heard from this man by way of the Talent. I have only second-hand knowledge—yet here I am in the middle of the forest, fleeing from everything I know. Where is he? I thought he was supposed to join us out here."

"He was," her father said. "I don't know what happened to him. It's quite possible he met with the very fate he warned us all against. If only we knew more about him, maybe we could learn if anything happened to him."

"I'm leery of this Rab," Dennel said. "Where did he get all his advance information? And why haven't we ever heard from him before?"

Komak shrugged. "I can't possibly answer those questions. Perhaps he comes from Mekk's fortress—maybe that's where he got his information. One thing we do know: his warning was timely and correct. Need I remind anyone of the slaughter we experienced second-hand on the third night after fleeing the keep, the slaughter we might have experienced *first*-hand were it not for Rab?"

No one met his searching gaze.

"I'm still suspicious," Dennel said finally. "How did Rab manage to contact those who were not publicly known to possess the Talent? Adriel is the only Finder in the province . . . I fear a trap, Komak."

"Well, if there's a trap, Rab will have caught himself—because he contacted us via the Talent, which puts him on Mekk's extermination list along with the rest of us. And there is something you all should know: There are still a number of Talents hiding undiscovered in Kitru's keep."

Dennel gasped. "There are? How do you know?"

"The morning after the slaughter, before we fled the area, I asked Adriel if she could pick up any traces of survivors." He turned to Adriel. "Tell them."

Adriel blushed and cleared her throat. "There were still a few left. Not many. Maybe four, certainly no more than six."

"Kitru has probably found them by now," Dennel said.

"Perhaps not," Komak said. "They may have been latent Talents, unaware of their gift, and therefore not publicly known as Talents."

"And to think," Dennel said morosely, "it used to be such a badge of pride to be known as a Talent. Now it's the equivalent of a death sentence."

Someone said, "Kitru will be nailed up outside

his own gates if Mekk should come across any Talents in the realm during his inspection tour."

"I'd love to see that!" said another.

Dennel said nothing.

"That won't help us, however," Komak said. "It's best we learn to like the forest. I fear it will be home for a long, long time."

On that depressing note, Adriel retired to her tent and verbal conversation ceased.

The tery considered what he had learned. The world of the humans was in turmoil. He sympathized with Adriel's plight but had little sorrow to spare the rest of them. He had too great a sorrow of his own, and humans were to blame.

He settled near the fire and tried to doze. He would need his strength for tomorrow. For tomorrow he would have to go back home.

IV

He was well enough to travel on his own the next day and slipped away from the train of the psi-folk as it moved deeper into the forest. He was not deserting his rescuers; he intended to stay with them, for he had nowhere else to go now and they seemed fairly well-organized.

The raw meat and milk of the night before, and again this morning, had restored his strength. Moving steadily, if not quickly, through the lush foliage, he knew where he was going and what he would find. He hadn't wanted to leave Adriel. It would have been so easy to stay by her side and leave all the pain behind. But he couldn't. He had to face the horror.

The hunting had been particularly good two days before. The tery hunted with a club. He was fast and strong, and could move as silently as an insect when he wished. A club was all he needed.

34

That day, he was early in returning to the clearing around the cave that served as home for him and his parents. He intended to surprise them with the two large *dantas* he had bagged. But it was he who was destined to be surprised: a squad of steel-capped, leather-jerkined strangers had invaded their clearing.

Keeping low, he had crept through the small plot where they tried to grow a few edibles. Halfway through the garden, the tery noticed something huddled among the corn stalks to his left. He crawled over to investigate.

His father lay there. A big, coarse brute who was happiest when he could sit in the sun and watch with eternal wonder the growth of the things his mate had taught him to plant. His eyes stared sightlessly from out of a face frozen in bewildered agony. He had been pierced by a dozen or more feathered shafts and the pooled red of his life was congealing on the ground beside him.

Rage and fear exploded within the tery, each struggling for dominance. But he dug both hands into the ground and held on until the dizzy sick feeling swept over him and passed on, leaving only the rage.

Then he grabbed his hunting club.

Holding it tightly, he kept low to the ground between the rows of stalks and moved slowly toward the cave, following the sound of human voices, hoping . . .

The soldiers stood around the mouth of the cave, laughing, joking, sampling some of the wine his father had been fermenting.

"I wonder where they stole this," one trooper said, his beard dripping purple fluid. "It's good!"

At their feet lay the tery's mother, her head nearly severed from her twisted body.

All control had shattered then. Screaming hoarsely and swinging his club before him, the tery charged. The utter berserk ferocity of his attack was almost as startling to him as it must have been to the soldiers. He heard their shouts of fear, saw the terror in their eyes as he leaped into their midst.

Good! Let them know some of the terror and pain my parents must have felt before they were slaughtered!

The archers were caught with their bows unstrung, but the troopers' swords were already bared and bloody. The tery didn't care. He wanted *their* blood on his club. The first of the group lifted his blade as the tery closed, but the creature batted it aside and swung his club for the trooper's head. The man ducked but not quickly enough. The club sank into his left cheek. Blood jetted from his nose, and the tery had one less opponent facing him.

Movement to his right. He swung again in a backhanded arc with most of his body behind it. The club connected with the shoulder of an archer, who went down screaming, then a two-handed blow into the throat of another swordsman.

For a moment, he had the advantage as they milled about and tripped over each other. The idea briefly danced in his head that he would kill them all and completely avenge his parents. But there were too many of them, and all were seasoned warriors. Before he could inflict any more real damage, the club was sliced from his hands and a sword point bared three of his ribs.

Wounded, weaponless, the tery ran. And he would have escaped easily had not the captain thought to order his men to their mounts.

"Don't run him through!" he heard the captain yell. "Just keep slicing at him!"

It must have been great sport. The troopers were all excellent riders. They would cut him off, then surround him and slice away. When each had added fresh blood to his sword, they would let him escape the circle and run a short distance, only to cut him off and start slicing again. He was an exhausted bloody ruin by the time he finally collapsed in a field of tall grass.

"Shall we burn him and the others?" he heard a trooper say.

"It will take too long," the captain panted as he stared down at the tery from his mount.

"But Mekk's decree is to burn—"

"We don't have time! Besides, if he's not dead now, the carrion eaters will finish him off! They do as good a job as fire, but they're slower!"

Laughing, they left him for the scavengers.

The tery remembered that captain's face.

The clearing was much as he had left it—except for the scavenger birds. He chased them away from the decomposing, partially devoured things that had been his parents.

Mother . . . Father . . .

His throat was thick and tight as he stumbled through the clearing. Until now, he had never realized how much he loved them, how much they meant to him, how much he cherished them. The thousand tiny kindnesses lost among the clutter of the daily routines, the caring, the worries for him—he had never appreciated these things, never realized how much they meant to him until it was clear that there would be no more of them. Ever.

Did they know? Did they know how much he loved them? Did they die unaware of what wonderful parents they had been?

At the risk of reopening some of his deeper wounds, he went about the task of placing the cadavers inside the cave. It was grisly work. The stench, combined with the knowledge that these rotting horrors were all that was left of the two beings who had meant everything to him, made him retch a number of times before the task was completed.

He rested to regain his strength, and thought of his parents, picturing them alive in his mind—he could keep them alive there, at least—and recalling their pasts which he knew by heart from the countless times his mother had sat him on her knee as a child and told him whence he came.

His father had been a wild, bearish creature, born of equally wild parents and raised in the forests where he had spent all his life. Yet he was a gentle sort, preferring berries to meat, and sleeping in the sun to hunting.

His mother was different in both appearance—no two teries were alike unless directly related—and social history. Graceful in a feline way, she had been captured as an infant and brought up in the keep when Kitru's father was lord there. That was in the time before Mekk issued his proclamation calling for extermination of everything that did not bear True Shape. It was considered fashionable then to have a tery or two around the court who could speak and recite.

His mother was one of those teries. She would delight visitors with her singing, her recounting of history, and the reciting of the many poems she had memorized. But in time, despite the luxuries around her, she tired of the empty existence of a pet, and escaped to the forests in her early adulthood.

There she met her mate, who could speak not at all and who could not learn to speak with any fluency—for although he had the intelligence, he had gone too long without ever speaking. He did manage to communicate in other ways, though, and soon a child was born to them.

The little tery's mother taught him to speak and taught him of his origin—how the Great Sickness had caused changes in many of the world's living things. His ability to think was one of those changes. These were things she had learned during her stay at the keep, and the cub absorbed everything she could pass on to him. He was bright, curious, and eager, and readily learned to speak, although his voice had a gruff, discordant tone.

He said nothing now, however, as he climbed the hillside above the cave and pried loose stone after stone until a minor landslide covered the mouth of his former home. When the rumble of the slide had echoed off into the trees and the dust had settled, he sat alone on the cliff and surveyed the clearing that had been home for as long as he could remember.

So heavy . . . his chest felt so heavy . . .like a great weight pressing down on him . . .

It was difficult for the tery to understand the turbulent emotions that steamed and roiled within his chest, making it hard to draw a deep breath without its catching halfway down. His placid life had not prepared him for this, and his emotions were in turmoil.

He had been wronged—*his parents* had been wronged! Injustice. It was a concept that had never occurred to him before, and he had had no experiences with it during his life. He had no injustices to draw on. For there was no justice or injustice in the forest, only the incessant struggle to go on living, taking what was needed and leaving what was not. Things tended to balance out that way. Carelessness was redeemed in pain and mishap, vigilance rewarded with safety and, often, a full belly.

More stealthy images crept unbidden from the past as he sat there. He had managed to hold them at bay while going about the task of interring his parents' remains, but now that that was done and he was gazing at the cold, dead, empty piece of earth that had once held warmth and security for him, he began to remember hunting and swimming lessons from his hulking father, and sitting curled up at his mother's side at the mouth of the cave in the cool of the evening.

His chest began to heave uncontrollably as a low, broken moan of unplumbed sorrow and anguish escaped him. He suddenly began to scramble blindly down the cliffside, nearly losing his footing twice in his haste to reach the clearing.

Once there, he ran from one end to the other, sobbing and whimpering, frantically casting about for something to break, something to hurt, something to destroy. As he approached the garden area, he grabbed one of the crude hoes his father had used for tilling and scythed his way through the stalks of maize and other vegetables growing there. When that was in ruins, he raced back to the base of the cliff and picked up any stones that would fit into his hands and hurled them with rage-fueled ferocity at the rubble-choked mouth of the cave. Some caromed crazily off the pile, others cracked and shattered with the tremendous force of impact. Whining and grunting, he threw one after another until a number of his wounds reopened and his strength was completely drained. Then he slumped to his knees, pressed his forehead against the ground, and released the sobs that echoed up from the very core of his being.

After a while, he was quiet. After a while, he could think again.

Another new concept for which he had only a name grew in his mind: revenge. Had his parents been killed for food by one of the large feline predators that roamed the forests, he would never have thought of retribution. That was the way things worked. That was existence in the wild. His parents would be dead—just as dead as they were now—but the balance would not have been disturbed.

The tery raised his head. Neither his mother nor his father had ever threatened or harmed a human; in fact, they had avoided any and all contact with them. Yet the soldiers had come and slaughtered them and left them to rot. Such an act was not part of the balance. It skewed everything, and nothing would be right again until the balance was restored.

The tery vowed to remember that captain's face.

He stood and surveyed the ruins of what had once been his home. He would cut all ties with the past now. From this day on, he was a fugitive tery and would stay with the fugitive humans he had met. His parents would be left behind, but he would not forget them.

And he would *never* forget that captain's face.

V

It was midday when the tery started back. The psi-folk would have been on the move all day, so he traveled on an angle to his earlier path in order to intercept them. He was moving along the edge of an open field when something made him stop abruptly and crouch in the grass. The skin at the nape of his neck drew taut and all his nerve endings buzzed with alarm as he sniffed the air for a scent.

Something had alerted his danger sense—his muscles were tensed and ready to spring, his jaw was tight.

Why?

His gaze darted across the field and in among the shadows around the bordering trees, searching for movement, for the slightest hint of a threat.

Nothing.

Taking a few hesitant steps forward, he felt the sensation increase. Fear . . . dread . . . forebod-

43

ing . . . they wormed into his brain and raced along his nerves. Yet he could find no tangible cause. Although his mind rebelled—*There is nothing here to fear!*—his legs moved him two steps backward of their own accord. Something within him—deep within him—was warning him away from this place.

He crouched again and strained his vision into the shade at the bases of the nearby trees. Perhaps one of the big meat-eaters had a lair there and a subliminal effluvium of death and dung was being carried toward him on the gentle breeze.

He saw nothing. Perhaps—

There! In the darkness between the boles of two large trees—something shimmered. It wasn't something . . . it wasn't anything, really. Just an area in the shadows about the size of a large hut that shimmered and wavered as if seen from afar through the heat of a summer day.

Keeping to the open field, he made a slow semi-circle, at all times staying low and maintaining his distance from the spot. It still shimmered, but he could see no more from the new angle and he saw nothing particularly threatening there. Unique and beyond anything he had ever experienced in his short life, yes—but nothing overtly dangerous.

Why, then, did it terrify him so?

He decided to find out. Slowly, with one reluctant step after another, he forced himself to approach the spot. And with each advance the terror within him grew, gripping him tighter and tighter until he felt as if lengths of vine were coiling around his throat and chest, suffocating him. His heart beat in his ears like a madman on a drum, the air pressed thick and cold against him. A cloud of impending doom enveloped him until his legs refused to respond to his mental commands, until his resolve shattered into a thousand screaming fragments and he found himself running, gasping, clawing his way across the open field, away from the shimmering fear.

When he finally managed to bring himself to a halt, he found himself on the far side of the field. He slumped against a tree trunk, trembling and panting while his sweat-soaked fur dried in the breeze.

He had never known such fear. Even when the troopers had chased him and sliced him and he had been sure he was going to die, he had not been so afraid.

What hideous thing hides there?

He waited until his heart had resumed its normal rate and he was breathing easily again. Then he moved away into the trees. He still wanted to know what lay within the shimmering fear and was determined someday to find out. There were many odd things left behind in the world after the Great Sickness, and the shimmering fear was certainly one of the most bizarre. Perhaps he could move through the upper levels of the trees and look down on it from above. That might work . . .

But not today.

He was too tired and emotionally spent today. All he wanted to do right now was to find the psi-folk, eat something, and settle near their central fire for the night.

Keeping the sun to his left, the tery moved further into the trees. He had not gone far when he came across an isolated hut. It was deserted. He noticed a kiln off to the side, cold, with clay pots and trays piled all around it. He looked inside the hut—clean, with a pallet on the floor and a small stone fireplace in the corner.

He guessed this must be the home and work place of the one who had found him after the troopers had had their sport. The man they called Tlad. The tery briefly debated whether or not to sit and wait for Tlad to return, then decided against it. He owed the man a great deal more than gratitude. But how to show it? From listening to conversations between Adriel and some of the psi-folk, he gathered that this Tlad was a solitary sort who did not make friends easily and had little need for the company of the other humans. He certainly would not want a tery around, then.

Better to leave now than impose himself on his rescuer.

The tery moved on through the forest, the only place where he truly seemed to belong.

As he continued toward the presumed location of the psi-folk, the physical and emotional stresses of the day were beginning to take their toll. Entering a grassy copse, he stopped to rest. A shift in the breeze brought the human scent and the sound of low voices from not far ahead.

He rose and hurried forward, but stopped abruptly.

Wait.

It was too soon yet to be intercepting the psi-folk, and idle chatter was certainly not one of their traits. Silently, he slithered along the ground to investigate.

A cluster of six humans was resting in the shade as their mounts grazed nearby. Leather jerkins . . . steel helmets . . . *troopers!*

All his fatigue suddenly evaporated in a rush of blinding hatred. But he held his position. He knew his reserves were low, and even under optimum conditions the headlong rush his emotions demanded would have been suicidal.

Cautiously, the tery circled them and continued on his way. His hour would come, he knew. He had only to wait. And besides . . . the captain was not among them.

He came upon the psi-people very shortly thereafter. For reasons not apparent, they had stopped their march early and were busily setting up their camp. Adriel spotted him first.

"It's the tery!" she cried, leaping to her feet and almost upsetting the mixing bowl in her lap. "He's come back!"

The other Talents briefly looked up, then went back to their tasks as Adriel rushed forward, fell to her knees beside him, and threw her arms around his neck.

"You came back!" she whispered as she hugged him. "They said you were gone for good but I knew you'd come back!"

Pleasant as this was, the tery had no time for such a welcome. He had just realized that the probable line of march of the scouting party would lead it close to this site . . . so close that discovery would be unavoidable. The troopers numbered only six, so there was no danger of an attack; but should they be allowed to return to Kitru's keep with even a general idea of the whereabouts of the psi-folk, extermination would swiftly and surely follow. He had to warn them.

But how?

He dared not speak for fear of letting them know he was a talker . . . *and* a thinker. That kind of warning would give away his reasoning ability. The tery could not be sure that their sympathy for his loneness in the vast forests would overcome their suspicion and reticence at having a talking, thinking, *comprehending* animal in their midst.

There had to be another way.

He broke from Adriel and ran to her father. Wrapping long fingers around the leader's arm, he tried to pull him away from the central pit he was helping to dig.

"Adriel!" Komak shouted, shaking off the tery's grip. "Get your pet away from me or we won't have a fire tonight!"

"I'll bet he's hungry," she said, and went to get some meat.

This approach obviously wasn't working. Short of a shouted message, only one recourse remained.

Bolting toward the trees, he ignored Adriel's pleading calls and disappeared into the brush. It didn't take him long to find the scouts—they were dangerously close and headed on a collision course. He searched the ground briefly and came up with a fist-sized stone, then climbed out on a limb that overhung their path and waited.

They were walking their mounts single-file through the dense undergrowth and grumbling about the heat and difficult traveling. As the last man passed below, the tery hurled the rock at his head and leaped from the tree. With a dull clank, the missile caromed off the trooper's steel cap and drove it into his scalp. His horse reared as the trooper sagged toward the ground. The tery grabbed the helmet off the lolling head and dove into the brush.

Hopefully, the loss of a man—whether temporarily or permanently, the tery could not be sure—would throw the scouts into sufficient confusion to allow the psi-folk time enough to prepare a move against them.

Gripping the rim of the helmet between his teeth and running as fast as his four aching limbs would carry him, the tery burst upon the campsite and went directly to Komak. The sight of a steel cap with fresh blood around the rim was all the big man needed to set him into action. He shot to his feet and glanced around. In an instant the camp was thrown into frenzied activity.

"What is it, father?" Adriel asked, aware that an order had been given.

"Troopers! Your pet's brought us a warning!"

"The tery?" She glanced his way with eyes full of wonder as her father guided her ahead of him toward their half-erected tent. "Good boy!"

"I never expected to see any of Kitru's men this far into the forests . . . but the tery was gone only a few minutes. They must be nearly upon us!"

She blanched. "What'll we do?"

"There's only one thing we *can* do." He bundled the tent fabric into a careless wad and shoved it out of sight behind a bush. "We haven't got time to run—although Dennel seems to think that would be the best course."

He glared across the clearing at the youth who stood uncertainly amid the flustration.

"We can't fight them!" she cried.

"We have no choice! Finding a recently abandoned campsite is the next best thing to finding the group itself. They'll run to the keep and soon a whole company will be charging after us. This is probably just a scouting party. All we can do is set a trap and hope there aren't too many of them."

The tents were quickly struck, and the women and children were sent from the clearing along with everything they could carry. Twenty men with strung bows concealed themselves in the surrounding bushes and trees.

"You come with me," Adriel said, gripping the fur at the nape of the tery's neck and tugging him along beside her. "It's going to be too dangerous here."

Reluctantly, the tery traveled with Adriel and the other noncombatants for a short distance, then pulled away. He doubled back to the campsite. He had to see what happened.

Komak's plan turned out to be fiendishly simple. As the tery watched from a nearby tree, the scouting party—one member rubbing a bare and bloodied head—entered the clearing in a cautious single file. They made a careful inspection of the half-dug central fire pit and conversed in low tones. The earth had been freshly turned and they were wary now.

The tery spied Komak watching from another tree. Why didn't he give the signal to shoot? What was he waiting for? They were all here!

Then the tery realized that Komak did not know

that. He was no doubt waiting until he was certain the entire scouting party had revealed itself.

The tery wondered what he would do in a situation like this if he had command of twenty Talent archers. Probably he would assign each archer a target trooper until each of the invaders was assured of three arrows; he would hold the remaining two archers in reserve. Then he would give the mental command to—

Suddenly came the *thrum* of many longbows loosing their missiles in perfect unison. Five of the scouts cried out as each was pierced by three arrows from three different directions. They lurched, twisted, fell, and writhed on the ground. The sixth had stooped suddenly to examine the grass and received only a superficial wound in the fleshy part of his upper right arm. Seeing the fate of his companions, he turned and ran for the brush. Two shafts from the reserve archers stopped him before he had covered six paces.

There had been no word during the entire episode, and no cheering at its close. If not for the cries of the dying, the rustle of the leaves, the noises of the birds and insects, the tery would have thought he had gone deaf. It dawned on him then that with greater numbers and a greater desire to fight, these psi-folk could rule the forests completely and pose a real threat to Kitru . . . and perhaps to Overlord Mekk himself.

Perhaps there was more than religion behind Overlord Mekk's inclusion of the Talents in the Extermination Decree.

The tery bounded out of his tree and scurried over to the dead troopers, hoping that these were the ones who had invaded his home and killed his parents. And even if they weren't, he wanted to gloat over them. After all, they were Kitru's men, and deserved the worst that fate could hold for them.

But when he reached the bodies and looked into their dead faces, there was no glee. He found he could not stare long at their frozen, agonized expressions. As vile and threatening as they no doubt had been in life, there was something pathetic about them now in death.

Feeling cold and empty, he moved slowly to the edge of the clearing and settled alone on the grass.

Before the women and children were brought back, the bodies of the troopers were carefully buried in the brush and their mounts added to the psi-folks'.

Adriel hurried ahead of the rest when they were told that all of the Talents had come through the skirmish unscathed and that it was safe to return to the campsite. The tery had run off again and she hoped he hadn't been accidentally caught in her father's trap.

She sighed with relief when she saw him sitting alone at the edge of the clearing. From his posture, it occurred to her that he looked depressed. But that was silly. How could an animal be depressed?

As they all hastily went about setting up camp for the night, she looked around for Dennel but he was nowhere in sight. She asked around but no one had seen him since Komak's decision to ambush the scouts instead of flee from them.

"Where's Dennel?" she asked her father. "Was he hurt?"

Komak grimaced through his beard. "Dennel? Hurt? Hardly. He ran off before our little encounter."

Adriel's heart sank. "I hope he'll be all right."

"He'll be back," Komak told her. "He can no more take care of himself than he can fight for himself. He needs us—we don't need him."

"He was always nice to me."

Komak put an arm around his daughter's shoulders and laughed. "For that reason alone, I'll welcome him back!"

"But is he really such a coward? He says he's mostly concerned with preserving the Talent."

"I know what he says. But I also know that he's scared to death."

"So am I!"

"I know. I'm scared, too."

"You are?" The idea shocked her. "You don't seem scared of anything."

"All an act, my dear. That's why I need all the help I can get. A short while ago when we set the ambush, I was supposed to have twenty-*one* archers. But one of them ran off. Dennel. Still running, I'll bet."

"Poor Dennel!"

"I know he's your friend, and I know you'd like to believe him about the possibility of the Talents coexisting with Mekk, but he's all wrong. Dangerously wrong."

"But he wants to preserve the Talent!"

Komak snorted. "So he says. He has this idea that we'd be better off if we split up into smaller groups. That way, in the event of an all-out attempt to do away with us, we could be fairly sure that some would survive to carry on the Talent."

"That sounds reasonable."

"On the surface, it does. But I really don't think Dennel's all that interested in preserving the Talent. Preserving Dennel is his main concern."

That remark stung Adriel, but she said nothing.

Komak paused, then grinned pointedly. "Besides —today proves that there are definite advantages to moving with a large group of individuals who can communicate silently and instantaneously. I think the lad just wants to run and I wouldn't worry too much about him. I'm sure he's not worrying about us. Your tery is a better friend— worth three Dennels."

Adriel turned and saw that her pet was now ambling on all fours among the psi-folk. Instead of ignoring him or swatting him when he got in the way, they smiled at him, called to him, scratched his back, or gave him bits of food. He had become a hero of sorts and had earned his place in the tribe.

"You're going to have to come up with a name for him," Komak said. "I'm surprised you haven't already."

"I wasn't sure he'd stay. In fact, I was almost sure he wouldn't."

"Well, it looks like he's going to be around for a while, and we can't just keep on calling him 'the tery.'"

"I'll think of a name, but I want it to be a good one."

"Fine. We should do what we can to bind him to us. He's proven to be a valuable watch animal."

"Don't you think it was strange how he warned us?" she said, watching the creature.

"How do you mean?"

"It was almost as if he knew we were in danger from the troopers and brought that steel helmet to warn us."

Komak laughed. "He might be smart, but he's not that smart! No, I think he showed a natural response to the merciless treatment he received at the hands of the troopers when they had cut his flesh to ribbons the other day. The tery came upon the scouts and instinctively attacked one of them, bringing back the helmet as a trophy."

"But he brought it right to you."

"Many pets do the same. No, the good thing about your tery is that he hates and fears Kitru's men as much as we do, but his senses are much keener than ours. He'll spot them long before we can."

"I guess you're right," she said, but she couldn't shake the feeling that there had been a definite *purpose* in her pet's actions today.

They broke camp early the next morning and began to trudge still deeper into the sun-filtered forest. Dennel had not yet shown up.

"Don't worry," her father assured her. "He'll catch up to us. We'll bring along his tent for him."

The sun was tangled in the trees by the time they stopped that day. Some of the psi-folk didn't even bother to set up their tents, but ate small amounts of dried meat and fell asleep under the stars. A light drizzle awoke them next morning.

It was a tired, cold, achy group that held a silent conference in a tight knot near the central fire. Finally Komak broke away and strode angrily to where Adriel sat with the tery. The group gradually dissolved behind him.

"What's wrong, father?"

"They want to stay here. We should be moving further away from the keep than this, but the women are tired and the children are crying and it was the consensus that this is far enough."

"I'm tired, too."

"We're *all* tired!" he snapped, then softened. "Sorry. I told you I never wanted this job. But one thing I'm going to insist on is sending out a few scouts of my own to see what the surrounding area is like before we get too settled."

VI

"Food . . ." she said in a plaintive voice, holding a small piece of meat before her. "Come, now. Say it: *Food . . .*"

The tery said nothing. Instead, he merely stared back at Adriel. He liked looking at her. He liked her freckled nose and the red highlights in her blond hair.

The sun was halfway to its zenith and Adriel had been coaching the tery since breakfast. She was nothing if not persistent. The girl seemed determined to teach her new pet to speak.

The tery debated the wisdom of giving in. Something deep within him ached to please her, to make her smile. He finally decided to gamble on a single word. Just for her. He pretended to follow her persistent example.

Feigning great effort, he rasped, "Food."

Adriel froze in wide-eyed wonder.

"Food," he repeated.

Komak was sitting nearby and turned his head at the unfamiliar voice. "Was that . . . ?"

"Yes!" Adriel said breathlessly. "It was him! He spoke! Did you hear him? He spoke!"

She quickly gave the tery the piece of meat she had been holding and held up another. But further demonstration of his newfound ability was halted by the arrival of one of the point men Komak had sent out.

After a few moments of telepathic conversation, her father turned to her.

"Looks like we'll be needing you."

"Oh?" She seemed to have been half-expecting this.

"Seems there's a tiny village a little ways off to the east. Perhaps twenty or thirty inhabitants, and one or two may have the Talent. It's up to you to find them."

Twelve mud-walled domes sat in a circle around a wide area of bare earth. Adriel motioned the tery to stay back out of sight in the brush.

Tense, not knowing what to expect, she walked toward the circle of huts, holding tightly to her father's arm.

"Hello!" Komak called when they entered the circle. "Hello, inside! We come in peace. We wish to speak with you!"

Slowly, one by one, the inhabitants of the minuscule village came out of their huts and stared curiously at the newcomers, whispering and pointing, but saying nothing to them, and not straying far from their doorways.

Adriel left her father at the perimeter and pro-

ceeded to the center alone. He couldn't help her
with this. Only she could find the Talent.

No one understood the Talent, least of all Adriel.
Her mother, before she had sickened and died,
had tried in vain to explain it to her. Half of the
Talent was another voice, she had said, a separate
voice that did not automatically accompany vocal
speech. It had to be volitionally activated and
projected. The other half was the receptive faculty
that operated continually unless it was consciously
blocked out. Most Talents learned of their ability
first through the receptive facet.

Adriel understood none of it. She could neither
send nor receive. The Talent was little more than
a tingling in her mind, a vague sensation she could
home in on and almost touch. To those who possessed the full Talent, reception was nondirec-
tional. Images appeared behind their eyes, words
sounded between their ears, concepts exploded
within their minds. But from where?

Adriel knew where. And that was why she was
here. To see if any of these villagers belonged with
her group.

Adriel closed her eyes. The Talent was strong
here! She could feel it!

She turned in a slow circle. Once. Twice. Then
stopped and opened her eyes again. She faced a
man, a woman, and what looked like a ten-year-
old boy.

There was a faint, familiar sensation of the Talent off to her right that she knew was her father.
There was another sensation, a strong tingling in
the forepart of her brain, emanating from the trio
before her. She moved forward and the sensation

became stronger with every step until she stood within arm's reach.

The man was blank, but the woman and boy were definitely Talents. Strong ones. She placed one hand on the woman's shoulder and the other on the boy's head, then looked at her father.

The two Talents followed her gaze to Komak and that was when he contacted them. With a reassuring smile beaming through his red mane, he motioned them toward him.

"What do you want?" said the uncomprehending husband, glancing nervously between Adriel and her father.

"It's all right, I think," the woman whispered. "Let's go with her."

The trio followed Adriel to where her father waited.

"Now tell us what this is all about!" the woman demanded sharply when they were out of earshot of the village.

"We mean you no harm," Komak said.

"We'll see about that!"

Her manner was suspicious and hostile. Her features were pinched and her jet hair was drawn back severely. Adriel decided she didn't like her much.

The woman added, "And use your tongues so my husband will understand!"

"They're Talents?" her husband asked.

"Yes! And I pray they haven't given us away!"

"Then you know of the danger," Adriel said.

She nodded sadly. She looked terribly frightened now and Adriel's feelings softened for her.

We're all afraid.

"We're traveling with a group of Talents," Komak said, "the only survivors after Kitru slaughtered all the rest of our kind in the keep. We want you to join us. We number fifty-three now and need every Talent we can find."

"Why?" the woman asked.

"For safety, of course. Overlord Mekk will be visiting the keep, and Kitru has been scouring the forests for teries and Talents in preparation for his arrival."

The man shook his head. "We'll stay right here."

"That could be dangerous," Komak told him. "What's to prevent some of Kitru's men from coming through your village with a Finder and ferreting out your wife and child as we did? He'll show no mercy."

"We're isolated out here," he said. "Almost lost. I've been to the keep two or three times in my life and nobody there even knew this village existed. And no one here knows that my wife and son possess the Talent except me. I think we can risk staying where we are."

Adriel was disappointed to hear that, for their sake—and her own. At least with the husband around, she'd have someone to talk to.

"Very well," Komak said after a pause. "We'll be camped toward the sunset for a while, if you should change your minds."

"Thank you," the man said. "But the forest nomad life is not for us. We'll take our chances here."

He put one arm around his wife and the other around his son as the trio walked back to their hut.

"Isn't it rare for a psi to marry a non-psi?"

Adriel asked her father as they returned to the forest.

"Very rare. The rapport between two lovers with the Talent is far and away more intimate than anything a non-psi can experience. But the woman and her son were the only psis around so it's possible she never had a lover with the Talent. She doesn't know what she's missing." His eyes seemed to glaze as if he no longer saw the forest through which he was walking.

"I wish them well," she said at last in an attempt to bring her father back from his reverie. "It must take a lot of courage to stay put in that little village and risk extermination."

"Or a lot of foolishness. The dividing line isn't always clear."

VII

It wasn't until four days after the ambush that Dennel returned. The tery had sensed his approach for some time before he appeared, but Adriel was the first of the humans to spy him. She ran up to him. The tery followed close behind.

"Dennel! You're back! How'd you find us?"

He did not meet her gaze. "I followed the mental chatter."

"Are you all right?"

"I think so," he said. He seemed very uncomfortable. "I . . . I have to find my tent. Excuse me."

"Poor fellow," Adriel said as she watched him walk away. "He's so ashamed for running away."

The tery wondered if it might be something else, but he had little opportunity to find out. Dennel kept to himself for the next few days.

Adriel and the tery were fast becoming inseparable and took little notice of Dennel or anyone

63

else. He let her "teach" him more words and she devoted most of her day to him, resting her hand on his back and talking to him as they wandered side by side through the leafy glades near the camp, chattering her heart out.

"I know you can't understand me," she said, speaking to him as if he could as they sat on a grassy knoll and watched the brightly colored tree-things go about their daily routines, "but at least I know your ears are for me alone. I know you aren't secretly carrying on a mental conversation with someone else while I'm talking to you."

The tery gathered that was something that had happened more than once in the past.

"You're lucky, you know," she told him. "Nothing holds you down. You can come and go as you please and you're at home with us or away from us. But me . . . I'm stuck here with a bunch of people who feel insulted if they have to use their tongues!"

She laughed. "I thought I was going to be a fine lady once—can you believe that? A nobleman's son took a fancy to me and I thought I'd someday be living in the upper levels of the keep. Then Mekk went and issued his new decree and I've spent the past few months living like a savage."

The tery came to think of Adriel as a wonderful creature—yet he pitied her. She was fresh, young, ready to burst into womanhood at any moment, and only a fanged, barrel-chested beast at her side to share the experience. She wanted to love and be loved, to stop running: she longed for the stability she would have had had she not been born a Finder.

He desperately wished there was a way he could help her.

As the days went on, the tery became a substitute for everything she desired. A thousand tiny kindnesses were showered upon him. She would put extra time and effort into preparing the meat for his dinner, and she carved and painted a bowl from which he could eat it. She learned the use of the loom so that he wouldn't have to sleep on the bare ground.

The two were driven closer and closer together by the void of silence that separated them from the rest of the tribe. Life became an idyll for the tery, a series of sun-soaked days of easy companionship . . . until the morning by the river when he discovered a dark and frightening hunger lurking within him.

Adriel was modest by nature. Every morning she would retrieve a jug of water from the stream that passed not too far from the camp and sponge herself off in the privacy of her tent. This particular morning was an exception, however, for she left the jug empty and led the tery along the bank of the stream until it widened and emptied into a river.

Pushing through the brush, she stepped down the bank and up to her ankles in the water. The far shore was further than the tery could throw a small stone, but floating leaves moved by at a leisurely pace, indicating a gentle current.

"There," Adriel said with a self-satisfied air, "I knew we'd find a river eventually. This looks deep enough."

She pulled off her blouse and the knee-length

pants she had recently made after finally deciding that a skirt was impractical in the forest. She wore nothing underneath.

Without the slightest hesitation, she made a shallow dive into the clear water, then bobbed to the surface and turned to face the tery.

"Ohhhhh, that feels good!" She dunked her head again and came up gasping. "I thought I was never going to feel clean again!" She motioned to the tery. "Come on—jump in! It's only water!"

But he stayed behind the bushes lining the bank. That much water made him uneasy. He had often waded to his knees while fishing with his father, but the thought of immersing himself to his neck was frightening.

And there was something else . . .

The brief glimpse of Adriel's nude form had stirred something within him, something pleasurable and yet uncomfortable. He stayed where he was.

Adriel splashed the water in front of her.

"Oh, come on in! You'll like it! Really!" But her pet made no move to join her. "Looks like I'm going to have to drag you in," she muttered and kicked her way closer to shore.

When she reached the shallows again, she stood up and waded toward the bank. Her skin was white and smooth and glistened wetly. Water ran from her hair over her rounded, budding, pink-tipped breasts, down across her abdomen to the red-gold fuzz that covered her pubes.

The same pleasurable something washed over the tery again as he watched her. It was a warm something that seemed to be centered in his groin.

She was completely out of the water now and climbing the bank in his direction. The warmth in his groin increased and the erratic fleshy part of him that usually hung awkwardly between his legs became large and stiff. His breathing was rapid as he tried to look away, but he could not.

This was wrong! He wanted to leap upon her, paw her, press the hungry distended flesh into her . . .

Wrong!

Adriel leaned over the bushes and extended her hand to him. "Come on," she said in a coaxing voice. The sunlight caught the myriad droplets of water that had formed on her bobbing breasts, and the cooling effect of a gentle breeze had caused her nipples to harden and stand erect. "I won't let you drown."

With an abrupt motion he wrenched himself around and tore headlong back into the trees. He kept running, concentrating all his physical effort on moving his four limbs as fast as his muscles would allow. Leaping over fallen branches and around earth-sunk boulders, he raced past Tlad's empty dwelling, across the field that bordered the shimmering fear, and didn't stop until he stood in the ruined clearing that had once been his home.

Exhausted, he slumped on the rubble-choked mouth of the cave that held his parents' remains and wished for them to rise and live and comfort him. Life had been so much simpler then. His mother had had all the answers. She would explain this blazing turmoil within him, explain why a tery should have such an unnatural desire for a human.

He waited, but his mother did not rise.

As his strength returned, so did memory of Adriel's glistening naked form, reaching for him. He felt the warmth return, felt himself grow erect again. Enclosing the stiff, enlarged member within both of his fists, he began moving them up and down until a spurting spasm brought a relief of sorts.

The tery returned to the psi-folk camp in the late afternoon. He did not approach Adriel's hut immediately as he would normally do, but wandered the perimeter, wondering if she knew what had happened down by the bank.

Guilt and fear gnawed at him. What if she guessed his feelings? She'd be shocked and repulsed. He couldn't bear the thought of losing her.

Near the center of the camp he saw a cart loaded with pottery. Tlad was here. He searched for the man and found him squatting beside Komak in the shade, dickering.

"Then it's settled," Tlad was saying. "A hindquarter of *ma* for the load. And fresh—none of this dried stuff."

"Agreed," Komak nodded. "You drive a hard bargain, Tlad. You'd never get such a price if we hadn't broken so much pottery in that forced march we had to make from the old campsite." His eyes narrowed. "But what I want to know is how you found us here? We've come a long way since we last saw you."

"I've lived in the forests longer than you. I have ways."

"I'm sure you do. But we waded down a stream most of the way. We left no trail."

Tlad shrugged. "I have ways."

Komak broke off further interrogation when he caught sight of the tery loping toward them.

"Looking for Adriel?" he said, rising and affectionately roughing up the fur at the back of the tery's neck. "She told me about you—afraid of the water, are you? Well, we're all afraid of something, I guess."

Afraid of the water. So that was how Adriel had seen it. Relief flooded him.

"Where is Adriel, anyway?" Tlad asked. "I want to ask her a few things about this pet of hers."

The tery looked around to find Tlad staring at him. The man's penetrating gaze made him uncomfortable. He looked away.

"Good question," said Komak, his lips tightening into a grimace of distaste. "Off walking somewhere with Dennel. Don't know what she sees in him."

"You don't think too much of him, I take it?"

"I like him not at all and trust him even less. But that is a problem between Adriel and myself. As for you—there are a couple of hunting parties out now. Should be back with a *ma* or two by sundown."

Tlad nodded. "I saw one of them setting up on my way here. Think they'd mind if I watched?"

"Just stay well back and quiet and out of sight," Komak warned and strolled away.

The tery was about to follow Komak in search of Adriel but was stopped by Tlad's voice.

"They tell me you're a hero around here now,

eh? Coming up in the world. Komak says Adriel's even managed to teach you some words. Isn't that interesting?"

He squatted before the tery, putting their eyes on the same level. The tery held his gaze this time.

"Tell me, tery," he said. "Are you really a dumb animal? Or are you playing games with these folk?"

The questions made the tery uneasy. Tlad seemed to know more than he should. He felt his gaze wavering. He growled and turned away.

The man rose and mumbled a few unintelligible words, then walked off toward the trees. Looking over his shoulder as he moved, he slapped his thigh once and called to the tery.

"With me!"

The tery hesitated, unused to being commanded to do anything, and not liking it. But Tlad intrigued him. And since he lacked anything better to do at the time, he drew up alongside Tlad and kept pace. He felt strangely drawn to the man. The fact that he had been instrumental in saving his life was an important factor, but there was a feeling of kinship with Tlad, a certain undefined sharing of a common ground.

They moved side by side through the forest until Tlad suddenly stopped and motioned the tery to stay where he was. Alone, he moved cautiously and silently ahead, briefly disappearing into the undergrowth, then returning with a satisfied smile.

"Want to see how your friends the Talents hunt?"

The tery almost answered, but stopped himself just as the words reached his lips.

"Follow me," Tlad said. "And be quiet."

Without a word, he chose a tree and began to climb. The tery followed. When they were five or six man-heights up the tree, Tlad made himself comfortable on a limb. Shielding his eyes against the late afternoon sun to his right, he peered ahead in the direction they had been traveling.

The tery followed the line of his gaze. When he spotted the object of all this attention, he nestled into the corner of the branch just below Tlad's and set up his own watch.

In a small clearing, eight Talents—five men and three women—stood in a semicircle with arms linked. No one moved, no one made a sound. They stood that way for what seemed an interminable period. The tery began to get restless. What was this all about?

"Be patient," Tlad whispered. "It will happen soon."

The man continued to watch in silent fascination.

Despite Tlad's advice, the tery was about to climb back down to the ground and find something more interesting to do when he noticed a movement in the brush surrounding the clearing. The head of a large buck *ma* appeared. The tery froze where he was and stared.

Slowly, hesitantly, the *ma* moved forward until it had fully emerged from the brush. *Mas* were vegetarians —grazers and leaf-nibblers—and their only defense against the carnivores that craved their flesh was speed. A graceful neck held the creature's snouted head on a level with those of the Talents who faced it; a sleek, short-furred body tapered down to four delicate legs. *Mas* were skittish and bolted at the slightest provocation, which made the sight of one standing not five paces from a group of humans almost incomprehensible . . . unless the Talents were exerting some sort of influence over the beast.

The *ma* continued its cautious forward movement until it stood within the semicircle. It appeared to be half asleep. Then with one abrupt motion, the male Talent on the near end of the semicircle raised a heavy club and brought it down against the slim, sloping neck where it joined the skull. The *ma* crumpled, instantly, painlessly dead.

The men were lifting the hind legs in preparation to drag it back to camp when suddenly all the Talents froze in their places momentarily, then dropped whatever they were doing and ran back toward the camp, leaving their prize game animal where it had fallen.

"This looks bad!" Tlad said and started to scramble down the tree. "Something's wrong!"

The tery followed him to the ground, but once on all fours, he left Tlad behind as he raced for the camp. He found chaos, with silent, grim-faced people running in all directions, grabbing weapons and harnessing mounts. He immediately looked for Adriel and could not find her. A chill of foreboding stole over him as he hunted up Komak.

He finally found him at the weapons wagon, filling a quiver with arrows. The tery hesitated, fearful for Adriel, yet unable to learn a thing about her.

Tlad arrived then, puffing from the run, calling for Komak. The big red-haired man ignored the call and strode toward his tent without answering.

Tlad, however, would not be put off. As the tery watched in the waning light, he intercepted Komak and matched his stride. After a brief exchange, Tlad stopped short and grabbed Komak's arm. They seemed to be arguing. Komak finally wrenched his arm out of Tlad's grasp and hurried away.

The tery approached Tlad, hoping he might learn something from him.

"There you are!" Tlad said. He squatted before him and put one hand on his shoulder. "Listen, my furry friend, and listen well: Adriel has been captured by Kitru's troops. No one knows how it happened but there are tracks to the south that show Adriel and Dennel walking right into the arms of a squad of troopers."

The tery felt as if he had been hit square in the chest with a battering ram. He couldn't breathe.

Not my Adriel!

He turned to head toward the keep but Tlad pulled his head back around and stared into his eyes.

"Listen to me! These fools are going after her— they have some crazy idea about storming the keep. That may be just what Kitru wants. Not only will he have a Finder in his control, but he'll be able to slaughter all the Talents who escaped from him when the proclamation first came through. *You*"—he slapped the tery's shoulder—"must get to the keep first. Get in there and get her out. I don't know how you're going to do it, but try! Not only does Adriel's life depend on it, but the lives of everyone in this camp. You owe them, and now it's pay-back time. Get going!"

The tery needed to hear no more. Without a

backward glance he turned and trotted into the trees, pacing himself for what he knew would be a long and dangerous journey through the darkening forest. With easy, loping strides, he left the scrambling psi-folk far behind. It was a long trip, and he would be there long before them.

He was well on his way to the keep before he realized that, without the slightest hesitation, Tlad had told him what had happened, what he should do, and why he should do it—*fully expecting him to understand every word!*

VIII

The keep was a darker blot against a darkened sky when the tery reached the edge of the forest. He stole through the narrow streets between the huts and houses that made up the village that surrounded it. The main gate was well-guarded and well-lit. Torchlight flickered off the guards and the metal fastenings of the gate itself, and off the rotting crucified corpses nearby, remnants of heretics and criminals and anyone else whose misfortune it was to displease Lord Kitru. The bodies hung and stank until they rotted off the spikes that pinned them there or until the spot was needed for a fresh miscreant.

The tery turned away and moved off into the darkness. Finally, far from the gate, he stood at the base of the high outer wall and gathered his strength and wits. He had never been in the keep before, but that didn't bother him—he had often hunted unfamiliar sections of the forest, and come back with game over his shoulder.

This would be like a hunt—the keep would be an unknown section of forest, the troopers would be the big predators with which he was always in competition, and Adriel would be the prey. He geared up his confidence. He could do this. He had been raised in the forest with a club as his only weapon—he either learned to use his strength with stealth and cunning or he went hungry. The tery had seldom gone hungry.

He began to climb. The outer wall was crudely made of rough stone, and his long fingers found easy holds as he scuttled upward. He reached the top, and raised his eyes above the ledge. There was a narrow walkway all along the outer wall with wooden stairs leading up to it. Sputtering torches and oil lamps placed at odd intervals within the wall showed a number of irregular buildings that made up the keep, one standing noticeably higher than the others.

A bored-looking sentry approached along the walkway. The tery lowered himself and hung by his fingertips just below the ledge until the guard had passed, then slithered over the top, dashed across the parapet, and dropped to the ground where he crouched in the deep shadow under the walkway.

With his heart pounding, he waited. No alarm was sounded, no troopers came running. He had successfully penetrated the first line of defense. The next step was to decide which building to search first.

His gaze was drawn to the tall, imposing structure that stood over the other buildings. That would be where Lord Kitru would reside—it seemed logical that a man who believed himself to be above other men would want to live where he could look down on them.

With neither weapons nor clothing nor accouterments, the tery was a fleeting shadow among other shadows as he made his way to the base of the tower. Yes, Kitru would dwell here. And who would better know the location of the captured Finder than the lord of the keep? Perhaps he had even quartered her here to assure her safekeeping.

He looked up the face of the tower wall. It was made of the same rough stone as the outer wall, so climbing it would be no problem. The surface was pierced here and there by narrow windows which the tery judged wide enough to allow him entrance. He started up. He had traveled only three man-heights when a shout from below caused him to freeze and hug the wall.

"Ho! You there on the tower! What are you doing?"

The doors to the trooper barracks flew open and there was the sound of many running feet in the darkness.

The same voice spoke again. "You! Come down from there! I've got a crossbow now . . . start coming down! No tricks or I'll split you with a bolt!"

Glancing up, the tery saw the lowest window not far above him. He made a sudden frantic leap to reach it. True to his word, the guard below loosed a bolt. The missile grazed the tery's ear and smashed against the wall in front of his face. Fragments of stone and mortar peppered his eyes. Recoiling, he felt his fingers slip off the stone.

Despite his best efforts, he lost his precarious grip and fell. He landed on all fours but found nowhere to run—the wall was to his back and two full squads of troopers faced him with drawn weapons.

"Someone get a light and let's see who we've got here!"

A torch was quickly brought and the troopers recoiled in surprise at the nature of their captive.

"It's one of those damned beasts!" exclaimed a burly guard with a pike. He drew the weapon back and the tery readied to dodge. "This'll finish—"

"*Stop!*" cried a voice from somewhere in the dark.

The troopers turned to see who had dared to tell them to spare a tery. A young man dressed in civilian clothes stepped into their midst with an imperious manner.

It was Dennel.

The sight of him walking free within Kitru's keep froze the tery in shock.

"Just who are you to be giving orders around here?" the man with the pike asked belligerently.

"Never mind that," Dennel said. "Just let me tell you that if this tery is killed, Kitru will have your head. This particular beast could be very valuable to him."

The trooper paused, uncertain, looking as if he were considering using the pike on Dennel. The tery sensed his resentment at being told what to do by someone he considered an unblooded, baby-faced, non-combatant upstart. But if this youngster were telling the truth, the trooper might well end up on the receiving end of Kitru's wrath—and that was not a place anyone wished to be.

He turned to the man beside him. "Get Captain Ghentren."

There followed a short period of tense waiting during which the tery put aside his surprise at Dennel's appearance and looked for an avenue of escape. There was none. The troopers formed a tight, impenetrable semicircle around him.

Half-dressed, his eyes puffy from sleep, the captain arrived and the tery felt an involuntary growl escape his throat. His body crouched to spring. He knew this man! This was the officer who had ordered his men to slice but not to kill . . . this was the parent-slayer!

One of the troopers who was watching him more closely than the others heard the growl and recognized the tery's stance. He raised his crossbow.

"Watch him!"

The tery forced himself to relax as the troopers pointed their bows and pikes at him, ready to kill at the slightest move. He would never reach the captain.

The officer glanced at the tery without the slightest hint of recognition in his expression, then turned to his men.

"This had better be important enough to wake me—I'm to leave on a mission for Kitru before the first light."

The burly trooper with the pike stepped forward and pointed to Dennel. "This whelp says Kitru will have my head if we kill the tery."

The captain turned to Dennel. "Oh, so it's you. Since when do you speak for the lord of the keep?"

"Because I know this beast!" Dennel replied. "It's the girl's pet and she's very attached to it."

"I care nothing about the Finder's pet!" he snarled and turned away. He threw a command over his shoulder as he began to walk away. "Kill the ugly thing and burn its filthy carcass in the pit."

"You'd *better* care about the Finder's pet!" Dennel shouted.

The captain whirled, rage blazing in his eyes. "You watch your tongue or I'll have it removed!"

"I—I'm sorry, sir," Dennel said quickly. "But I'm only trying to be helpful. The Finder is immensely important to Kitru. He can try the drugs first, but if they fail, he'll need a lever to get cooperation from the girl. This beast might just be that lever."

Drugs? the tery thought. *What are drugs?*

But the question was washed away in the rush of anger that followed the realization that Dennel had been a party to Adriel's abduction—had planned it, perhaps!

The captain was pondering Dennel's remarks. The tery silently urged him to find some advantage in keeping him alive. For the tery now had two scores to settle.

"If the drugs work on the Finder, you can burn the tery at dawn or whenever you wish," Dennel said to the captain in a low voice. "But if the drugs fail—and I understand they are not too reliable— the tery might prove useful to Lord Kitru, and then you will be glad he is still alive. Then you can take full credit for his capture."

"Perhaps you are right," he said with sudden mildness. He turned to the troopers. "Take the creature below and throw it in with the crazy one. I think they'll make excellent company for each other!"

This brought a laugh from all the men and broke the tension. Dennel turned and departed, a satisfied smile on his face.

"By Mekk's beard, who was that?" one of the pikemen asked as they watched him go.

"A coward and a traitor to his own kind," Ghentren replied in a low voice. "He thinks he's got Kitru's ear, but the lord told me himself that as soon as he has no further use of the whelp, I can do what I wish with him."

The tery saw the captain's smile and knew from experience what kind of torment it could spell.

A pikeman gave him a poke with the sharp end of his staff and he was prodded toward a sunken stairway that led under a building adjacent to the main tower.

"Below" consisted of a small underground chamber broken up into three tiny cells. It was apparent that there was little need for incarceration facilities at the keep. Executions were far more economical and certainly less time consuming. Sharp, jabbing pike tips herded him into the middle cell and the lone guard locked the door behind him.

Amid harsh barks of laughter someone yelled, "Company for you, Rab!"

The laughter faded as the tery watched the troopers file out. The guard reseated himself by the door and tried to doze. In the wan torchlight that filtered through the grate in his cell door, the tery rattled the door and tried to figure out why it wouldn't open. He had heard of locks, but had never seen one before. He was peering through the keyhole, trying to see the inner works, when a gentle voice startled him.

"You're a man, aren't you." It was not a question.

The tery whirled to see a filthy, bearded, bedraggled man standing behind him, watching him intently.

"I can tell by the way you examine that lock that you're more than just an intelligent animal."

He looked old at first, but as he moved forward and came into the faint light from the hall, he appeared to be somewhere between youth and middle age.

"Can you speak?" he asked.

The question was so casual, it took the tery by surprise. The man's attitude reminded him of Tlad. He hesitated a moment, then realized that there was little point of hiding his ability from his cellmate.

"I can speak," the tery said in a slow, harsh, grating voice. "But I'm not a man."

It was odd, speaking to this human. He had never really spoken to anyone but his mother and father in his entire life. He had repeated words and sentences to make Adriel happy, but that was hardly speech.

"Oh, you're a man, alright," the dirty one said, looking the tery over carefully. "It's just that nobody ever told you so. My name's Rab, by the way."

"The troopers called you 'crazy,' " the tery said pointedly. "Twice."

"And I must look the part, too!" Rab laughed. "But anyone who's been locked up in a hole for months without a bath, clean clothes, or decent food will start to look a little crazy"—his voice lowered briefly, almost as if speaking the next phrase to himself—"and perhaps even *feel* a little crazy at times"—then rose again—"but I assure you I'm not! And I also assure you that you're quite as human as I am."

The tery snorted. "Do not play with me. I may not be human but neither am I a fool!"

"But you *are* human!"

"I know what I am: I'm a tery, a product of the Great Sickness."

"And I'm a doomed heretic for knowing that you're not!" Rab shouted angrily.

The tery turned back to the lock. The soldiers were right. This man was insane.

Rab eased his tone. "Sit down and let me tell you what I've learned. You'll find it hard to believe because it goes against everything you've been taught since birth. But I can prove it—at least I could when I had my books. Sit. We've got plenty of time."

The tery was not so sure of that. Yet, what else could he do? He had tried the door and knew it was proof against even his strength. The conversation he had overheard between Dennel and the captain had eased his fears about Adriel being in any immediate danger . . . and perhaps this deranged human could help him if humored.

"Please?" Rab said. "*Please?*"

No human had ever said that word to him. Reluctantly, he eased himself down onto the damp, straw-littered floor.

"Good!" Rab said, squatting opposite him, rubbing his filthy hands together. "First off, I've suspected since my early youth that the tery is not the mutated beast tradition tells us he is. In fact, I more than suspected it—I knew it."

"How could you 'know' it?"

"Never mind how. That's not important now. Let it be enough for the moment that I did."

"Everybody knows that teries were a product of the Great Sickness after it swept across the world."

"No-no! That's not true. Listen. You'll see. I was raised a scholar in Overlord Mekk's court and had the training and time to search into the past. I found old manuscripts from as far back as the time of the Great Sickness. Our language has changed much since then but I did manage to decipher them and found many references to a group of people called 'the Shapers,' and 'the Teratols.' Just who they were and what they did was never explained. It seemed to be taken for granted that the reader knew.

"All this whetted my appetite for more, so I searched deep into the caves and ruins that surround Mekk's fortress. In one I chanced across some old—very old—volumes. They were lovely things, different from all the others, in perfect condition, printed on incredibly thin sheets of metal . . . five volumes . . . you've never seen anything like them . . ."

His voice trailed off as he briefly seemed to relive the find, a scholar's ecstasy beaming through the grime and matted hair that covered his face. Then he shook himself and resumed his tale.

"Yes . . . five volumes. I finished translating four of them a few months ago and was so caught up with what I'd learned that I ran to tell Mekk himself."

He paused and smiled grimly. "That was a stupid thing to do—for that act alone I deserve to be called Crazy Rab. I didn't get to see Mekk, of course. No one gets to see the Overlord these days since the True Shape priests took over as his advisors. I was shunted off to one of the high priests and should have had sense enough then to keep quiet. But no! Crazy Rab had to lay the entire translation out before the high priest. I was so excited about what I'd found that I never considered what a threat it was to the political power the True Shape cult had acquired."

The tery listened with growing interest. If the True Shape cult felt threatened by Rab's discoveries, perhaps there was something to them.

"You see, I had learned some incredible things in those volumes. I learned that we are just a tiny colony of a larger race, that our ancestors came from the sky and that there are hundreds of other colonies of humans scattered all over the other side of the sky."

"Madness!" the tery growled.

"It sounds crazy, I know, but those volumes are real and obviously not a product of our culture."

"But to live on the other side of the sky!"

"It seems that our ancestors were banned from the mother world and settled here to build their own culture. They were called 'Shapers' and toyed with the stuff within that gives a thing its shape, that makes a child resemble its parents. They set out with the mission to create a perfect race of perfect humans, each with the power to speak mind-to-mind; the Talents were the high point of the Shaper art.

"But it didn't last. A perverted element, the Teratologists or 'Teratols,' as they came to be known, came to power and a being's shape became a plaything for the ruling clique. They created monstrous plants, made beasts look like men and men look like beasts."

"Teries were caused by the Great Sickness," the tery repeated.

"Not true. That's a myth. Someone like you and someone with The Talent are *both* human, and both are *teries!*"

"Then you are saying that Overlord Mekk is right in lumping Talents together with teries."

"Yes! Both are products of the Teratol regime."

"And where is this regime now?"

"Dead. Gone. Wiped out in the Great Sickness. In fact, the five volumes I found were apparently written at the height of the Great Sickness. Their author says in the fourth volume that the Teratols accidentally caused a change in something called a 'virus,' and a monstrous plague swept the world, reducing our ancestors' civilization to rubble. We are the survivors."

The tery regarded his fellow captive thoughtfully. The man did not rave—seemed quite sane, in fact—and spoke with utter conviction. But it was all so preposterous, so contrary to common knowledge! Everyone knew . . . and yet, if those volumes truly existed . . .

"Where are the volumes now?" he asked.

"Kitru has them. It's a complicated story involving incredible stupidity on my part. But briefly: In Mekk's fortress, the high priests tried to get the volumes from me. They were ready to kill me to silence me, but first they wanted those books.

"So I fled, but not before learning of the proposed addition to the old Tery Extermination Decree that would mark all Talents for extinction. I took the volumes and came here, hoping to find someone in power who would listen. I went to Kitru with my translation and he threw me out. I'm ashamed to say that I went back again and that's when he had me thrown in here to await Mekk's arrival, which has been twice postponed—thankfully. So I've moldered for months. When the Overlord finally does arrive, I'm to be nailed up by the gate as a heretic."

The tery shuddered at the thought of hanging in the sun to die of thirst and starvation while the crows and vultures waited to get at your eyes. Better a quick, clean death.

Rab sighed despondently. "At least I managed to warn the Talents of the new extermination decree. Most of them fled to safety in time."

The tery's mind made a delayed correlation: "You're Rab!" he said in an excited growl.

"Yes. I believe I told you that a number of times."

"You're the one the psi-folk have been waiting for!" He had heard the name mentioned many times among the Talents but had failed to connect it with this man.

"How do you know that?" Rab asked, rising slowly to his feet.

"I've been living with them. But that must mean—"

"Yes . . . I'm a Talent. And a Finder, as well. But Kitru doesn't have a Finder of his own so he does not know that I'm either."

"But he does have a Finder!"

The tery briefly recounted the day's events.

Rab was frantic. "You mean the Talents are coming here? Now? They'll be wiped out!" He began to pace the perimeter of the tiny cell. "We've got to stop them!"

The tery remained seated in the center of the cell and watched Rab move around. "Can we dig out?"

Rab stopped pacing and shook his head. "No. The keep is built on solid rock. The only way out of here is through that door."

The tery returned to the door and rattled it again.

"Too strong," he said.

"You know," Rab said slowly, "I never had the opportunity to get the advantage on one of these guards when I was here alone, but now that there's two of us—and only one of us thought to be human . . ."

IX

The dozing guard at the outer door was startled to wakefulness by shrill cries of fear and pain from the central cell. Grabbing a torch from its wall brace, he rushed to the door and peered through the grate. The flickering light revealed the tery in ferocious assault upon the screaming Rab.

The guard hesitated briefly, then decided it might be wisest for him to intervene. Kitru only imprisoned those whom he thought might prove useful at some time in the future. And such must be the case with Crazy Rab. Even though it hadn't been his idea to put the two of them together, if the prisoner were killed, the guard knew he would end up crucified outside the gates instead of Crazy Rab.

Unlocking the cell door, he entered with the torch held before him. His plan was to back the tery away from Rab and then drag the man out and put him in a separate cell.

"Back!" he yelled, thrusting the torch toward the tery's face. "Back, you ugly beast!"

The tery looked up and shrank away from the flames, releasing the moaning human.

"Don't like fire, do you?" he said, pressing his advantage. "Didn't think you would!"

What he didn't expect, however, was that Crazy Rab would leap to his feet and grab his sword arm. The guard turned to strike at the human with the torch but felt it wrenched from his grasp by the tery who had suddenly lost his fear of fire. In one motion the tery lifted him into the air like a child. Suddenly he was tumbling through the air toward the stone wall.

As the guard rolled to the floor and lay still, Rab bent over him, then rose and regarded the tery uneasily.

"He's alive, but barely. I think you broke half his ribs. You're quite as strong as you look, my friend, but you'll have to learn a little restraint."

The tery replied with a low growl. He wanted to find Adriel and could not concern himself with the well-being of those who would harm her.

"I'll show them as much restraint as they showed my parents."

"Oh. I see. I'm sorry."

"Find Adriel," the tery said impatiently.

Nodding, Rab led him from the cell.

"She must be in the tower. I became acquainted with this area of the keep fairly well while awaiting audiences with Kitru and I think I know how we can gain the stairs of the main tower without being seen. After that we'll have to depend on luck."

the sound of coherent speech from the lips of what he had considered a stupid beast, coupled with the naked fury he saw in that beast's yellow eyes, would have struck him dumb.

"Easy, now! Easy!" Rab said, ascending into the light. "Just hold him steady. He's a Talent and I'll communicate with him that way to save us time."

Dennel locked pleading eyes on Rab, obviously looking for a way out of the tery's grasp. But Rab's expression remained cold, his eyes flinty, until he had learned the answers to whatever questions he was asking.

"All right," he said finally. "Set him down and he'll lead us to the Finder."

The tery complied and hovered impatiently over Dennel as the young man leaned against the inner wall, gasping and rubbing his throat. Rab pushed him upward.

"Move. It'll be light soon."

Dennel took two steps, then lurched away and started to run down the steps. The tery caught the back of his tunic in his fist and raised Dennel into the air again. He was about to hurl him against the stone steps when Rab caught his arm and stopped him with an urgent whisper.

"*No! Put him down!*"

The tery hesitated. He wanted to hurt this human, and he could see in Dennel's wide, terrified eyes that he knew it, too.

Rab stared hard at Dennel. "He won't try anything that foolish again—will you?"

Dennel shook his head. The tery hoped the human was now fully convinced that he was not quick enough to elude the tery's reach.

Rab scrutinized the tery as he put Dennel down. "You frighten me, friend."

"You have nothing to fear from me," the tery said in a rough whisper. "Only the captain named Ghentren and those who would hurt Adriel need fear me."

Rab's smile was wry. "That's a relief."

The tery pushed Dennel between them and pointed upward. "Lead."

Rab paused before moving. "I think I'd know you were human now even if I hadn't found those ancient volumes. Since we entered this tower you've displayed craft, deceit, loyalty and outrage at betrayal. For better or for worse, my friend, you're as human as I am."

The tery pondered this in silence as a thoroughly cowed Dennel led the ascent. Following almost absently, he tried to sort the confused jumble of thoughts within his mind.

Could Rab be right? Could he be truly human after all? Was it really so preposterous?

He thought back on his brief co-existence with the psi-folk and realized that he had so easily accepted their company, as if it were the most natural thing, despite the fact that he had had no previous close contact with humans. Not only had he felt at home with them, he had been drawn back to them after initial contact. He didn't need them for food or shelter—he simply enjoyed being in their company.

Perhaps the desires awakened in him by Adriel the day before were not so unnatural after all . . .

Further speculation was terminated by Rab's hand on his shoulder. They had reached the top of the stairway and a great wooden door barred their way. Hearing a voice within, Rab elbowed Dennel aside and gently pushed it open.

A lean, graying man stood in the center of the room, a wine cup in his hand. He was dressed in a soiled tunic girded with a leather belt from which hung a short sword in a scabbard.

The tery heard Rab mutter, "Kitru."

The lord of the keep swayed as he poured red liquid from a silver flagon. Adriel was bound to a chair before him, her back to Rab and the tery.

Kitru was shouting at the girl. "Fool doctors! Told me the drugs would make you totally subservient to my will—idiots! I wasted the entire night waiting for them to work!"

The tery froze for an instant at the sight of Adriel, then coiled to lunge forward. Rab grabbed his shoulder and signaled him to wait. The tery eased back. He would wait—but not much longer. He watched Kitru sip noisily from his cup and go on speaking to Adriel.

"But when it's light and I've had some rest, we'll try a new approach—the howls of your beloved pet should make you more compliant. And if that fails, we'll make sure to capture your father alive when he arrives to save you. But I *will* have a compliant—no, *enthusiastic*—Finder by the time Mekk arrives! Do you understand me?"

The tery dropped all caution then and burst into the room. Startled by the intrusion, Kitru instinctively reached for his sword. The blade was out of its scabbard by the time the tery reached him, but before it could be put to use, the tery knocked it from his hand and closed long fingers around the keep lord's throat.

"*Don't!*" Rab cried. "I know what you're thinking, but *don't!* Just hold him there until I check the girl."

He leaned over Adriel. The tery watched her face. Her expression was blank, her pupils wide. Rab shook her shoulder and her head lolled back, but she did not respond.

The tery growled and tightened his grip on Kitru's throat. Rab turned quickly.

"She's all right. I've seen the effects of this drug before. She'll be like this until about midday, then she'll be sick, and after that she'll be herself again."

Above the tery's constricting fingers, Kitru's face was turning a mottled blue.

"Let him go for now but watch him—we'll use him for safe passage through the gate."

"Who are you?" Kitru rasped as he slumped to the floor and clutched his bruised throat.

"Remember the man you called 'Crazy Rab' and threw into the dungeon?" Rab said with an edge on his voice as he untied Adriel. "I was a much more presentable member of humanity then, but beneath this beard and filth I am that same naive scholar."

"How did you get up here?"

"The same way we'll get down," Rab said, untying the last knot. "The stairs." He rose to his feet. "There! Now, where are my books?"

Kitru jerked his head toward a dark corner of the room. "But only four remain."

"I know," Rab said, striding to the indicated spot. "Dennel tells me you've sent one off to Mekk with news that you have a Finder. Your messenger will be wrong on both counts—when Mekk arrives there will be no books and no Finder. And he won't like that at all."

"Ah! Dennel, is it?" Kitru said, his eyes coming to rest on the young man cowering in the doorway. "You have a knack for betraying *everyone*, it seems."

"No sire! I swear—they forced me into this . . ."

His voice trailed off as he sought but found no hint of understanding in Kitru's face.

The tery glanced at Adriel slumped in her chair. She looked . . . dead. He took a step toward her, just to check—and that was when Kitru made his move. With a quick roll he grabbed his fallen sword and gained his feet. The tery pivoted to find a gleaming length of sharpened steel hovering a finger's breadth from his throat.

"Rab," Kitru said with a tight smile on his face, "you're not only crazy, you're a fool as well. You should have fled when you had the chance. I'll see you nailed up outside the gate at first light, while your traitorous Talent friend and this beast are roasted alive in the tery pit."

"No!" Dennel cried.

The lord of the keep seemed to have lost all trace of fear now. The tery wondered why. Was it because he considered himself a good swordsman, and all that threatened him here were an unarmed scholar, a coward, and an animal? Perhaps his confidence had been further bolstered by the wine he had consumed.

The tery prepared to attack at the first opportunity.

"We are leaving with the girl," Rab stated coolly.

"Oh?"

"Yes. This fellow"—he indicated the tery—"is a friend of hers. He's going to take her back to her people."

Kitru laughed aloud. "Friend? Oh, I'm afraid you're crazier than anyone ever imagined, Rab! This is her pet!"

"*I am a man!*" the tery said and Kitru took an involuntary step backward.

The tery was not quite sure why he had said it; he could not truly say he thought of himself as a man. The declaration had escaped him involuntarily.

"You're not a man!" Kitru sneered after recovering from the surprise of hearing words from the beast's throat. "You're nothing but a filthy animal who can mimic a few words."

"How strange," Rab said in a goading tone. "I was just thinking the same thing about you."

In a sudden rage, Kitru roared and aimed a cut at the tery's throat, figuring to catch the beast off guard and then dispose of the other at his leisure. He lunged wildly, however, and the tery leaped aside and aimed a balled fist at the back of the keep lord's neck. Kitru went down without a sound and lay still, his head at an unnatural angle.

Rab came over and nudged the body with his toe.

"I wish you hadn't done that. I was going to trade his life for safe passage out of here."

"There'll be no safe passage for us anywhere now!" Dennel wailed.

"We can still get back to the forest," Rab told him.

"The forest! What good is that to me? It's a living hell out there! I can't go back there!"

"If the other Talents can manage, so can you."

"I—I'm not like the others. I can't live like an animal, scrabbling about for food and shelter. The forest has always scared me. I'm frightened every day out there, every minute. I can't eat, I can't sleep."

"But out there you live as a man," Rab said. "Here, you live as a tool, and you're allowed to do that only so long as you prove yourself useful."

"No—you don't understand." A thin line of perspiration was beading along Dennel's upper lip. "I can reason with them . . . make them accept me!"

Rab turned away. "Suit yourself." He indicated Kitru's inert form. "Think you can make them accept that?"

The tery had already forgotten Kitru and was kneeling beside Adriel. The girl stared vacantly, unseeingly ahead of her, but did not appear to be physically injured. The tery lifted her, one arm across her back, one under her knees, and held her tightly against him. She was breathing slowly, regularly, as if sleeping. It was strange and wonderful to hold her like this.

After a long moment, he turned to Rab.

"She will be all right?"

"She'll be fine."

Rab was busy wrapping the four remaining books in a wall drapery. Even from across the room the tery could sense something strange, alien about those volumes. Rab tied a knot, then carried them to the center of the room.

"*If* we get out alive," he said. "And I've got an

idea of how we might do that. If we can get downstairs unseen—"

"There is one debt yet due in this keep," the tery said.

He had tasted vengeance tonight and craved more. One more life needed to be brought to an end before the balance would be restored: The parent-slayer dwelt below in the barracks.

"What are you talking about?"

"A captain named Ghentren must die before I leave tonight."

"Ghentren left a little while ago," Dennel said from the doorway. "He was sent to Mekk's fortress with a sample of the books and news of the captured Finder. He's gone."

"Forget him," Rab said, swinging the sack of books over his shoulder.

The tery said nothing, but knew he could not forget him. Balance would not be restored until Ghentren's blood had seeped into the dirt like his mother's and father's.

Rab headed for the steps, pulling Dennel after him. "Come. We'll get you out of here alive."

The tery brought up the rear, carrying Adriel's limp form as gently and smoothly as possible. He kept his eyes on Dennel, directly ahead of him, watching him closely.

Why are we bringing this traitor with us? he thought angrily. He could not forgive Dennel for betraying Adriel. *If he wanted to return here so badly, why not let him stay?*

As they rounded a curve in the stairway, he noted a subtle change in Dennel's demeanor. The young man's slumped, dejected posture gradually straightened. He stole a quick glance over his shoulder at the now-burdened beast behind him. The tery sensed trouble brewing.

Then without warning, Dennel leaped for one of the window openings in the wall.

"Guard! Guar—!"

The tery's fury erupted. With one quick movement, his right arm snaked out and lifted Dennel into the air by his throat. He swung him in an arc and smashed the young man's head against the stone wall, cracking it like an egg. A grisly stain remained on the stones as he loosed his grip and let him drop.

Rab's face blanched. "Did you have to do that?"

The tery looked at the limp, twisted form and felt that the balance was a little closer to being restored.

"If his yelling brought the troopers, we'd all be dead," the tery growled. "Now only he is dead; we still live, and there are no troopers." He clutched Adriel closer. "If he wishes to be killed, he should not include us."

Rab sighed. "He didn't think he'd be killed. I caught a flash from his mind in the instant he called out—he thought he could use sounding the alarm as a show of loyalty. Poor Dennel. He feared the forest, and they wouldn't let him stay here."

Poor Dennel? The tery didn't understand. You were loyal to friends and family, you protected them against those who would harm them. Dennel had done none of those things. *Why Poor Dennel?*

Continuing the descent, Rab grabbed a torch out of its holder on the wall and led the way to the kitchen. The scullions had not yet arrived. Rab found the wood pile for the stove in a corner. He shoved the torch into it.

"What are you doing?"

"Giving Kitru's men something to worry about besides us."

That struck the tery as a brilliant idea, but he feared large fires. Everyone who lived in the forest did.

After assuring himself that the wood was catching, Rab went to a window and looked outside. The tery followed him.

The stars were fading and the sky was lightening beyond the wall. Pre-dawn.

"Good timing for us," Rab said. "It's that hour of the day when consciousness has ebbed to its nadir, when the man awake finds it most difficult to remain so, and when the man asleep is most inert."

The smoke from the fire had filled the ceiling space and was now moving down upon them. The tery's eyes began to burn.

Rab coughed. "Let's go."

Rab and the tery became two wraiths skimming across the courtyard to stand and wait in the shadow under the walkway on the outer wall, each with his own precious burden.

They did not have to wait too long—it only seemed that way. The tery kept looking at the lightening sky, knowing that soon the shadows would fade, exposing them. The initial whisps of smoke from the kitchen went unnoticed. It was not until the flames caught the door and licked upward that a groggy sentry sounded the alarm.

All available hands rushed to quench the conflagration. As a bucket brigade was formed from the well to the kitchen, Rab and the tery crept up the steps to the parapet. Rab threw his books over the side, then reached for Adriel.

The tery held her, unwilling to let her go.

"I'll hold her while you go over," Rab said. "Hurry!"

Reluctantly, the tery gave her over, then scurried down the outer wall. Reaching the ground, he lifted his arms, feeling his heart beating in his throat. If he missed her . . .

Rab dropped Adriel over the edge and the tery caught her. He put her down briefly to catch Rab, then he had her in his arms again.

"Now run!" Rab whispered. "Somebody's sure to spot us before we reach the trees, so run like you've never run before!"

The tery found the going difficult. He was built to travel on all fours, yet with Adriel in his arms he had to run in an upright position. Her weight threw his balance off, but he still managed to outstrip Rab in their race for safety.

They were halfway to the trees when a call went up from one of the few sentries remaining on the wall. Before many arrows could be loosed, however, they were out of accurate range for even the best of the keep's archers. The trees closed in on them and they were safe.

After putting a little more distance between themselves and the keep, Rab called for a halt and dropped his bundle of books to the sward.

"I don't think there'll be much pursuit, if any," he panted, leaning against a tree trunk. "Once they find Kitru dead, there'll be nothing but chaos in the keep."

The tery stood with Adriel still in his arms, barely listening, his mind racing. Rab's voice trailed off. The tery felt his eyes on him, flicking over Adriel and the way he held her.

"Why don't you put her down and we'll see if we can bring her around."

It was a while before the tery could answer. He was lost in the sensation of Adriel's inert form against his chest as he clutched her there, tightly, possessively. Her warmth, her softness, her scent . . . all awakening a timeless ache deep within him. He had never been so close to her. Holding her like this . . .

He had come to a decision.

"That won't be necessary," he told Rab in a dry voice.

"What's that supposed to mean?"

"We're not going to rejoin the psi-folk. We'll find a life of our own in the forest. I'll protect her, provide for her, and no one will ever harm or threaten her again."

Rab's expression was sad. "I don't think that would be wise," he said softly.

The tery spoke in a rush, as much in an effort to convince himself as Rab.

"I'm human, am I not? You told me so yourself."

"Yes, but that doesn't mean—"

"Right now I feel *very* human! She's human, too. And she's lonely and unhappy living with the psi-folk. I could make her happy. She loves me— she's told me so, many times."

"She loves you as a beast! As a pet!" Rab said,

straightening and approaching the tery. "But will she love you as a man?"

"She will learn!"

"You don't know that! It's a choice that only she can make. And if you take her away and try to make it for her, then you're no better than Kitru and the captain who killed your parents!" His voice softened. "And there are some hard facts you must accept: If by some wild chance she did accept you as a man and a husband, the offspring of your bonding would carry your shape—or much of it."

The idea startled the tery. He hadn't thought of children. He envisioned horrid mixtures of Adriel and himself. They left him speechless.

"Your ancestors were deformed at the whim of some diseased mind. This atrocity has been perpetuated for generations. It might be best for you to decide to bring the Teratols' colossal joke to an end—let it go no further than you."

Anger and bitterness thickened the tery's voice as he spoke.

"I would find that easy to say if, like you, the only mark I carried was the ability to speak with my mind—a *gift* rather than a deformity! It is easy to speak of letting the curse go no further if someone else must make the sacrifice!"

A grim smile played about Rab's mouth. "Why do you think I've spent most of my life looking for a link between teries and humans? I told you I knew there was a link—how do you think I knew?"

"*You?*"

Rab nodded. "I was born with a tail, as were my mother and brother and sister, and their mother before them." He shook his head sadly. "What

amusement my ancestors must have provided some
depraved Teratol! Normal in every way except for
a scaly rat's tail!"

The tery sensed the pain and humiliation in
Rab's voice. It echoed his own.

"So, you're a tery, too."

"Yes. But for generations my family has seen to
it that the tail is cut off flush with the body immediately at birth—there's virtually no scar left if
done that early in life. And so they have passed for
all those generations as humans, yet all the while
thinking of themselves as teries, lower life forms
somehow altered by the Great Sickness so that
they looked and acted like humans. I'm sure some
of my forebears suspected that they might be human, but none was ever so sure as I. For I had
another birthright besides a tail—I had the Talent.
Neither my mother nor my father was so gifted—
perhaps each carried an incomplete piece of the
Talent within, and those pieces fused into a whole
when I came to be. I don't know. There's so much
I don't know! But I did know I was a tery with the
Talent, and only humans had been known to possess the Talent. So I decided to prove I was human."

"What has this to do with me?"

"I also decided that the Teratols have laughed
long enough. I shall father no children."

The tery stood unmoving, eyeing Rab intently.
He had known the man only a short while but had
come to trust him. He sensed he was telling the
truth. Yet he could not bring himself to put Adriel
down. He felt he would explode if the did not
have her. He *had* to take her away with him!

"You cannot stop me, Rab," he said finally.

"That's true. You've killed two men tonight, nearly killed a third. You could kill me easily. But you won't. Because I sense something in you, something better than that. I sense in you most of the good things that are human. And you won't force yourself upon the girl who befriended you."

The tery swayed. The forest seemed to reel and spin around him. He so wanted to be an equal in Adriel's eyes, but he never could be if they stayed with the Talents. What should he do? What was the *right* thing to do?

Rab emptied his ancient metallic volumes from the drapery that had served as a sack, and spread it on the ground. He stared at the tery expectantly.

After a brief, tense moment, the tery gently placed Adriel on the cloth and folded it over her. Feeling a sob building in his throat, he straightened and started to move toward the forest depths.

"Where are you going?"

"Away. I don't belong here."

"Yes, you do!" Rab said. "Or at least, you will. You'll be a hero among the Talents!"

"I'll still be a pet!" What had been so amusing before seemed intolerable now.

"You don't have to remain one."

"You'll tell them?" Hope began to grow. "Explain to them?"

"I'll help you become a man in their eyes. The Talents won't accept you as one right away, and they may even reject you if we push your humanness on them too forcefully. So we'll start slowly. You'll talk more and more; you'll start to use tools. I'll guide you. Before I'm through I'll have them thinking of you as a man before I ever get around to telling them! And the first thing to do will be to give you a name."

The tery turned and watched Rab's eyes as he spoke. Only one other man had ever looked at him that way.

Rab held out his hand. "Will you stay . . . brother?"

The tery looked away and said nothing. Moving slowly, almost painfully, he returned to Adriel's side. Lowering himself to his knees, he slumped and hung his head over her, wondering what to do. He remained in that position for a long time. He sensed Rab moving away to sit quietly with his back against a tree.

The tableau was broken by the sound of someone crashing through the underbrush nearby. Both were on their feet immediately: Rab half-hidden behind the tree trunk, the tery crouched over Adriel, ready to spring.

A lone man broke into view.

It was Tlad.

X

Tlad stopped at the edge of the clearing and stared at Adriel's inert form.

"Is she hurt?"

The tery sensed real concern in his voice.

"No," Rab replied, cautiously stepping out from behind his tree. "Just drugged. Who are you?"

"I'm called Tlad. The tery here can vouch for me."

Rab glanced sharply in the tery's direction. "He knows?"

The tery nodded—a very human gesture he had picked up—and lowered himself to all fours next to Adriel.

"He is a good friend. I don't know how he knows, but he does—perhaps for a long time. Maybe he is a tery, too."

The tery was beginning to feel the physical, mental, and emotional strain of the night's events. His mind and body were numb. A great weight

109

seemed to be pressing down on his chest and
shoulders, making it hard to stand; he barely noticed. Everything was coming apart. He wanted to
lie down and let it all pass. He felt adrift . . . lost
. . . stripped of his identity. His place in the world
had been torn away from him: He was no longer a
tery, he was a human. But he could neither live as
a human nor be accepted as one. Nothing added
up. He knew Tlad should not have been able to
find them, yet he had. The tery did not have the
will to wonder how.

Not so Rab, who had regained his composure
and was wasting no time in satisfying his curiosity.
His voice seemed to echo down a long tunnel to
the tery.

"How did you know to look for us here?"

"I have my—" Tlad began, but stopped short.

"Is something wrong?"

But Tlad did not answer. Instead, he rushed to
where the ancient volumes had been spilled from
the drapery and knelt to inspect them in the growing light.

"These are yours?"

"Yes."

"Where did you find them?"

"In the ruins near Mekk's fortress when I lived
there."

"Then you must be the one the Talents have
been waiting for. Rab, isn't it?"

"Yes, but you're not one of us."

"Right." Tlad continued speaking as he flipped
through each of the volumes. "But they're not far
behind me. They're heading directly for the keep.
I suggest you let them know where you are. They
should be in range."

Rab looked off into the forest for a moment, then returned his attention to Tlad.

"There. They know we're safe and where we are. Should be here soon. Now, tell me wh—"

"Where's Volume Five?" Tlad said in an agitated voice. He quickly ran through the four volumes a second time. "Did you lose it?"

Rab sat down with a jolt on the other side of the pile of books, a dumbfounded expression on his face.

"Who are you? I'm the only one who can read these things! How could you know that Volume Five is missing? This is the only set!"

"Wrong," Tlad replied. His voice was low, his words hurried. "I come from a fishing village but never had much of a bent for the sea. So as a boy I used to comb the ruins up the coast. I found a similar set and brought it to the village elder who knew how to read some of the ancient writing. He kept the books for a long time, and when he was finally through with them, he made me row him out past the reef. As we sat in the boat, he swore me to secrecy and told me what the books contained. Then he threw all five overboard."

"Then this is not the only set!" Rab said.

"No. And there may be others."

"This means you know about the Shapers and the Teratols, and the truth about the Talents and the teries."

"I also know the contents of Volume Five."

"Then you know more than I do," Rab said. "I never got to translate that one."

"Then it's lost?"

"No. One of Kitru's officers is on his way to Mekk's fortress with it now."

Tlad shot to his feet. *"NO!"*

The violence of Tlad's reaction startled Rab and even managed to penetrate the mental fog enveloping the tery. He rose and padded toward the pair.

"What's in the fifth volume?" Rab asked.

Tlad hesitated, then seemed to reach a decision.

"Volume Five tells of the final days of the Teratol society and how they gathered all their records, their techniques, and their hardware into a huge underground cache. Among the items they hid were the superweapons they used to keep the underclasses in line. Volume Five gives the location of that cache."

Rab, too, was on his feet now. "And it's on its way to Mekk!"

"If that madman gets his hands on those weapons, there won't be a forest left to hide in. He'll have everything that doesn't bear True Shape— whatever that happens to mean at the time—hunted down and destroyed. And a lot of other things will get destroyed along the way. Maybe everything. Is there any way we can intercept that officer?"

"No," Rab said with a quick shake of his head. "Dennel told me that the messenger was scheduled to leave during the night. He's long out of reach by now."

"Dennel?" Tlad said. "Where is he?"

Rab explained what had happened inside the keep.

Tlad nodded and glanced the tery's way. "I suspected Dennel was up to no good."

"He's not important now," Rab said. "I must know: Where is the cache?"

"Right under Mekk's fortress, if the maps were accurate. The Teratols seemed to think it was pretty safe—you had to go through the Hole to get to it."

Rab started. "The Hole? Then it's unquestionably safe."

"Surely the Hole is empty now!"

"No. The offspring of the original inhabitants still dwell there—no one dares to let them out. And no one enters the Hole willingly. Don't worry: The cache is safe."

"I wouldn't count on it. If Mekk learns that the Hole stands between him and the power to destroy anything that displeases him, he'll find a way around it or through it. He'll get to that cache."

"Then we're doomed!"

"Not if we get there first!"

"And they call *me* 'crazy!'" Rab said with a humorless laugh. "How do we do that?"

Tlad tugged at his beard. "I can't say. I'm from the coast. I don't know much about Mekk's fortress."

"You certainly know your way around the forest!"

"I live in the forest now—I'm a potter, not a fisherman. But there must be some way we can get into the fortress and retrieve that book."

"There is none, I assure you. Mekk dwells in mortal fear of assassination—that's why he's postponed his inspection tour of the provinces so many times. The walls of his fortress are sheer and high—not even our tery friend could scale them."

"How about the main gate? There's got to be traffic in and out of the fortress."

"All civilians must have passes to enter the fortress, and all are sent home at dusk. Mekk's tower is surrounded by troopers day and night. There are no chinks in his armor. I'm afraid we're lost."

"No," Tlad said with a certainty that seemed unfounded, "we're not lost. Every stronghold has at least one weak spot. I'll find it."

He turned and walked off into the trees.

The psi-folk arrived soon after Tlad's departure, and it was a silently joyous event. They all recognized Rab by his Talent and crowded around him, slapping him on the shoulders and back. Adriel was laid on a drag and had regained consciousness by the time they all returned to the camp area that evening. Rab, Komak, Adriel, and the tery sat apart during the celebratory feast that followed.

"This is quite a fellow you have here," Rab said, indicating the tery, who had not strayed from Adriel's side during the entire journey, and now listened intently to the conversation.

"That he is," Komak agreed.

Rab made sure to impress upon all the importance of the tery's role in Adriel's rescue. He pressed the point again.

"I can't say it often enough: If not for this fellow, Adriel and I would still be locked within the keep, and the rest of you would be dead at the base of the walls."

"I know," Komak said. "I never thought he would amount to much when Tlad convinced me to bring him into the camp, but he's certainly proved me wrong. He's a smart one—smarter than some humans I've known!"

"Is that so?" Rab said, his eyes dancing as a smile showed through his freshly washed and trimmed beard. "And you say Tlad was responsible for bringing him into camp?"

"You know Tlad?"

"We've met. A most interesting man. I'm anxious to meet him again. We've many things to discuss. But getting back to our friend here—do you have a name for him, Adriel?"

The girl shook her head carefully; she had complained of a throbbing pain in both temples since awakening.

"No. I was waiting to find a name I like for him but never got around to deciding. He's always been just 'the tery.'"

"Then I shall take the liberty of naming him for you. Do you object?"

Adriel did not appear to be in a condition to object to much of anything.

"No. Go ahead," she said. "I could never make up my mind what to call him."

"Good!" Rab said, seizing the opportunity. "Then I shall name him *Jon.*"

"Jon is a man's name," Komak said. It was more of an observation than an objection.

"He shall be Jon, nonetheless."

Jon, the tery thought. He liked that name.

XI

Two days later, when Adriel was well enough to travel, Rab assumed the role of leader from Komak with the latter's grateful blessings.

"Which way shall we move?" Komak asked. He spoke aloud because Adriel was present.

Jon, the tery, hovered nearby, listening.

"Eastward. That will take us further away from Kitru's realm."

"But it will also bring us closer to Mekk's fortress."

"I know," Rab said.

"Is that safe?"

"Don't worry, Komak. I fully intend to keep a respectful distance between our people and the Overlord's legions. But I'm formulating a plan. It's not fully developed yet. When it is, I'll let you know all the details. Trust me."

"You know I do. We all do."

Later, when Rab wandered off to a secluded

116

spot where they could meet and talk, Jon asked him why he hadn't told the Talents about the cache under Mekk's fortress.

"I don't want to frighten them. Some of them may panic and scatter. That will serve no purpose. We must stick together . . . and we must have a purpose. Our days of blind flight are over. Our future is tied to what lies hidden under Overlord Mekk's fortress. So we've got to deal with the problem of Mekk now or spend the rest of our lives on the run."

"How?"

"I don't know . . . yet. But I sense that our enigmatic friend Tlad will find that elusive weak spot in Mekk's defenses. And when he does, he'll need help. I want us to be nearby to supply that help."

"Why does Tlad want to help Talents and teries?" Jon asked. The question had been troubling him.

"I don't know. Do you trust him?"

Jon nodded. "I owe him my life."

"Then you have good reason to trust him. I have no such reason, yet something within tells me that the fate of the Talents is in some way tied to Tlad and—stranger still—to you, Jon."

Jon was startled. "What can I do?"

"I don't know. But I feel constrained to keep all the pieces at hand until the puzzle can be solved. But as to the here-and-now," he said, shifting the subject, "I notice you've been avoiding Adriel."

"Yes," was all Jon would say.

Once he had assured himself that she was fully recovered from the drugs, he had kept his distance.

"She doesn't understand. I believe she's a little hurt."

"She will recover," he said and turned back toward the camp.

The tery stayed with the tribe during its leisurely eastward trek. He continued to avoid Adriel, however, forcing himself to ignore her hurt and spread his company among the rest of the psi-folk. He did so not only because Rab suggested it, but because proximity to Adriel had become so achingly painful.

He would walk beside one of the Talents for a while and pretend that he was practicing his speech. He'd point to an object and call it by name, or point and pretend he didn't know what to call it and induce the Talent to tell him. He was fully accepted by everyone now because of his heroic rescue of Rab and Adriel, and within a matter of days the psi-folk seemed to be subconsciously convinced that he was more of a burly aborigine than an animal. Everyone delighted in working with Jon to increase his vocabulary.

Jon hated it.

Before he had met Rab, it had been almost amusing to play the dumb animal. Now things were different. Now he found the role degrading. He wanted to *belong*, to be accepted as the thinking, feeling, rational being he was. He, too, awaited Tlad's return to give the psi-folk—and himself—a direction other than flight, a goal beyond survival.

Rab drilled the archers daily. The march would be stopped in mid-afternoon; after camp was set, targets would be raised. Some were suspended on rope with pulleys for practice against moving targets. Simultaneous volleys were rehearsed time and time again.

Jon often heard grumbling over sore fingers, arms, and shoulders, but the improvement in co-ordination and accuracy he saw was significant.

At sunset of the eighth day, Tlad walked into the camp.

He was immediately drawn aside by Rab. Jon the tery followed. He wanted to hear what was being planned and, as ever, knew that he liked being near Tlad.

"Well?" Rab said expectantly when they were out of earshot of the rest of the tribe. "Did you find anything?"

"Yes and no." Tlad looked tired and his voice was strained, as if he had recently been under great stress. "There seems to be no way to get into Mekk's fortress other than a full frontal assault, and you haven't anywhere near the numbers for that. Also, there's no way to get to the weapons cache other than through the Hole."

Rab's face showed his disappointment. "So far you haven't told us anything we don't already know."

"Have patience. I have these."

He unrolled sheets of paper covered with incomprehensible wavering lines.

"What are those?"

"Maps. I've been wracking my brain to remember the maps I'd seen in Volume Five, and finally managed to come up with some crude copies from memory. They give us some idea of what the area around Mekk's fortress looked like before everything fell apart during the Great Sickness."

"But that's all changed now."

"Right. But it shows us a way to get into the Hole without going through the fortress."

"The Hole? Who'd want to get into the Hole?"

"We do. So we can get to the weapons."

"Go through the Hole?" Rab said in an awed whisper. "No one goes through the Hole!"

"We have to. There's no other way."

"But it's impossible! We'll be torn to pieces!"

Jon broke his silence. "What is the Hole?" He remembered his mother mentioning it from time to time, but she would never explain anything about it.

"Mekk's fortress is built on the ruins of what used to be the headquarters of the old Teratol regime," Tlad said. "That was where they performed most of their shaping experiments. From what I can gather, all their failures, along with their special experiments, the ones they couldn't risk setting free, went into a sealed cavern below. The special teries were the ones they had shaped inside and out—deformed their bodies without, and drained off all decency, mercy, empathy and compassion from within. They let monstrosity mate with monstrosity in the Hole to form new and even more monstrous offspring. It's concentrated depravity down there."

"It's full of teries?" Jon said. "Why doesn't Mekk eradicate *them*?"

Rab laughed. "I'm sure he'd like to! And I wish he'd try! But he can't risk it. His troops won't go near the Hole and he'd risk a mutiny if he tried to force them. So he's left them alone."

Jon was struck by the irony of it: Mekk the tery-killer forced to live over a huge nest of teries.

"It's hell pure and simple in there," Rab said, visibly shuddering. "I once had a glimpse of its denizens through one of the grates that provide ventilation for the Hole."

"Apparently the Teratols enjoyed watching them," Tlad said, pointing to one of his maps. "And this is where they did it."

Rab and the tery crowded around. Rab seemed to understand the squiggles on the map, but they meant nothing to Jon.

"What's that?" Rab asked.

"A viewing chamber. They built an underground corridor with a transparent wall through which they could watch the goings-on in the Hole in safety. That corridor is our way to get to the Hole without Mekk's or his troopers' knowledge. From there it shouldn't be far to the cache."

Rab shook his head. "Do you know what you're asking? I don't care how near or far it is, it can't be done! The foulest, most depraved teries in existence live down there in constant warfare. The only thing that can bring them together is the sight of a normal human—they will act in concert to tear that human to pieces, then resume fighting over the remains!" He lowered his voice. "That is how vagrants and petty criminals in this region are executed—dropped through one of the grates into the Hole."

Tlad grimaced. "They throw people into the Hole?"

"Only those not important enough to crucify."

"Still, it's a risk that must be taken," Tlad insisted.

"Forget it! I can't ask anyone to go in there!"

"Then I can't help you," Tlad said angrily and turned to go.

Jon placed a restraining hand on his shoulder. "Wait. Perhaps a tery could reach these weapons through the Hole."

"No!" Rab said. "Not even you could survive in there, Jon!"

"I want to try." He realized that he wanted very badly to do this.

"Why? You're risking your life."

"It is my life."

Rab waited a long time before answering.

"It could work," he said finally. "But how could one man accomplish anything?"

"He could bring back a few weapons," Tlad replied, "and with those at hand, we could clear a path through the Hole—nothing could stand in our way—and get the rest."

Rab's eyes lit with growing enthusiasm. He put his arm around Jon's hulking shoulders.

"Brother tery, you're about to save the Talents once again!"

Later that night, Jon sat by the central fire with Rab and Tlad after the rest of the camp had drifted off to bed.

"Why must it be like this, Tlad?" Rab said softly. He had a pile of small pebbles in his hand and was throwing them into the fire one by one.

"You mean war?" Tlad shrugged. "It seems to be part of the human condition."

"Think so? I wonder. Why must we be out here in the forests struggling to stay alive while Mekk and his priests and his troops are in their fortress scouring their brains for ways to find and kill us?"

"The True Shape sect seems to be at the root of your problem."

"Ah, religion. I could think of a better way to use religion, I assure you! Besides numbers, our greatest disadvantage is that all the religious myths have been turned against us. The True Shape faith says that the Great Sickness was an act of God, through which He altered all those who displeased Him. Therefore, all those bearing the mark of the Great Sickness are offensive to God and must be eradicated."

"We're all afraid of the strange, the misshapen. Even you aren't sure your fellow Talents won't reject Jon once you tell them he's human."

"I know. But it used to be considered wrong to hurt or kill others. Then the True Shape priests wormed their way into Mekk's brain and convinced him to order the extermination of all teries. I guess it was inevitable that Talents would be added to the list. So now it's an act of devotion to go out and kill a tery or a Talent. Everything is twisted."

"I'm sure Talents were included in the extermination order for political reasons as well," Tlad said. "If Mekk is as suspicious and fearful as you say, he probably wanted to eliminate those subjects who could possibly plot against him without ever saying a word."

"I suspect that's true. But if the present is bad, the future could be worse."

"Worse?" Jon whispered, unable to stay out of

the discussion any longer. "What could be worse than the present?"

"Well, at this point the provinces are complying with the extermination decree out of fear of Mekk's wrath. But as time goes on, the practice of killing on sight anything that doesn't bear True Shape will become traditional and customary and routine. It will continue long after Mekk is gone because it is entwined with religious myth. How do we fight a myth?"

"With another myth," Tlad said, matter-of-factly.

Rab laughed. "Just like that? Another myth? Ah, if only I had that power! I'd create a religion that could bring us all together, not drive us apart. Or better yet, I'd do away with all religion and let us live for ourselves."

"That would be unrealistic. Myths exist because people want them, cling to them, need them. To supplant existing religions, you'll have to come up with a bigger and better god, one who could push the others aside, one who could implant the ideas that teries and Talents are every bit as human as the rest of us, implant it so deeply that it could never be uprooted."

"If I can get my hands on those weapons," Rab said with sudden intensity, "I'll show Mekk and his priests just how human teries and Talents can be!"

"Is that what you want the weapons for? To make yourself the Overlord?"

"No, of course not," Rab said quickly. "But we can use them to change things around to our benefit. We won't have to run anymore—from anyone!"

Tlad made no reply. As Jon watched him gaze

into the fire, he noticed a worried frown on his face.

Jon sought out Tlad the next morning and learned that he had departed at first light, no destination given. He struck off into the forest and made for Tlad's hut. It was mid-morning but he knew he could easily catch up. No human could move through the forests as quickly as—

He'd have to get used to classifying himself as human. He had come to accept that now, and he wanted the other humans around him to accept it. But Rab said go slow, go slow, go slow. So he did. But it irritated him more and more each day that he had to hide his intelligence. Previously taciturn by nature, he had now developed an insatiable urge to talk to other humans. But there was no one to listen. Rab was always busy or surrounded by Talents, and when Tlad arrived, he and Rab spoke of things that Jon could not understand, and so he was forced by ignorance to remain silent.

So now he sought out Tlad—who was human yet did not seem to require the company of other humans. Perhaps he would accept the company of a tery who desperately craved to be with another human on an equal footing. They were both aliens, outsiders, standing apart from the rest of the culture—Tlad by his own choice, the tery by heritage and decree of law.

Tlad was not at his hut, had not been there recently by all signs. Perhaps they had traveled different paths; the tery passing him on a parallel course. Jon waited for a while, then decided to scout through the area between the hut and the new camp of the psi-folk.

Eventually, he came to a familiar clearing. Looking to his left he saw what he had come to call the shimmering fear. And something else.

Someone was in the field. A man . . .

It was Tlad.

Jon watched him approach the shimmering fear. He moved quickly, steadily, like someone who knew exactly where he was going and was anxious to get there. He walked right up to the shimmer—and into it!

The shimmer enveloped him and he disappeared!

Jon ran forward with his heart thudding in his throat. Tlad was in danger and he had to help! But where was he? Had whatever hid inside the shimmering fear drawn him in and swallowed him? Or was Tlad immune to the fear? Was he part of it?

The questions fled unanswered from his mind as he felt the first tentacles of terror and revulsion coil around his chest and throat and begin to squeeze. But still he ran. He ran until he felt he could no longer breathe, until his legs became stiff and rigid. And when he could no longer run, he walked, slowly, painfully, forcing each limb forward until he entered the shimmer.

Suddenly the forest was gone. His vision shifted and melted into a blur. All that was left was the fear that buzzed around and through him. Still he forced himself on, one more step . . . one more step—

The shimmer was suddenly gone.

And with it, the fear.

He stood panting and sweating in a cool, odor-

less room that seemed to be made out of polished
steel.

Not three paces ahead of him sat Tlad, seated
with his back to him. He was staring intently at a
portrait of a man on the wall above him. Jon
opened his mouth to speak . . .

. . . but the portrait spoke first.

XII

I regret having to say this, Steven, but I'm going to have to turn down your request. As you well know, the Federation Defense Force intervenes only in certain strictly limited areas, and your request for intervention on Jacobi IV does not meet the narrow criteria set forth in the LaNague Charter. The imposition of a protectorate in this case would be at odds with the very purpose of the Cultural Survey Service, which is to preserve and promote human diversity. The psis you've described on Jacobi IV are well on their way to establishing a truly tangential society; intervention by an interstellar culture at this point would stifle them. Your talented friends will have to find their own way out of this predicament, I'm afraid. I wish them all the luck between the stars.

*You may help them, of course, but only
with the materials at hand.*

Good Luck, Steve, and out.

"Damn!" he said through clenched teeth as he
angrily cut off the playback.

No sense in running through it again. It was
painfully obvious that this was an irrevocable decision on the part of the higher-ups. He had expected a rigid, by-the-rules response, but that didn't
lessen his frustration.

"Of all the stupid narrow-minded—"

He turned and froze at the sight of the tery
standing in the lock, staring at him.

"Jon?"

"You live within the fear?" the tery said, a tone
of awed wonder in his gruff voice.

"The fear?"

He was so stunned by Jon's presence that he
didn't catch the reference.

"The shimmer—"

"Oh, that!" He realized that Jon meant the craft's
neurostimulatory repeller. "I use it to keep out
people and curious creatures. But how'd you get
past the field?"

"I thought Tlad was in trouble. I came to help."

He saw how Jon was still panting and trembling,
how his fur was soaked with sweat.

"You came *through* the field?" He was moved.
The field induced an almost irresistible flight response in the autonomic nervous system of any
mammal within range. It was very potent. It took
guts to get past it. "Thank you, Jon."

"But you are not really Tlad, are you?" Jon said.

For all his bestial appearance, this tery had such a quick mind. Dalt tried to match his quickness but could come up with no lie that would ring true enough to save his cover. He thought carefully before he spoke. The tery respected him, felt indebted to him—he had come through the fright field because he thought Tlad was in trouble. Why destroy that store of confidence with an obvious fabrication?

"No, I'm really Dalt. Steve Dalt."

"But you are still my friend, are you not?" Jon asked with a pleading innocence and sincerity that Dalt found touching.

"Yes, Jon," he told him. "I'm still your friend. I'll always be your friend. I'm here to help the teries and the psi-folk, and I'll need your help most of all to do it."

Jon was staring around at the ship's interior.

"Can we leave here? I don't like it here."

"Of course. But first . . ." Dalt reached a hand toward the tery's right shoulder and removed a fine silver thread. "You won't be needing this tracer any more. I planted it on you before you went to Adriel's rescue. I've got them here and there among the psi-folk. Helps me keep track of things."

He laid the thread on one of the consoles, then picked a small disk from a slot by the lock and placed it in the tery's hand.

"Hold onto this as we walk through the 'fear.' It will protect you from it. I've got one in my belt buckle."

Together they walked undisturbed through the shimmer that protected Dalt's craft visually, and the neurostimulatory field that guarded it physically. They stopped in the shade of some neighboring trees.

Dalt sat cross-legged on the grass and motioned for the tery to join him.

"Get comfortable and I'll tell you all about myself. After I'm done, hopefully you'll know enough to want to keep what you've just seen a secret."

"As long as it helps Adriel and the others."

"Good enough."

Where to begin? he thought. *This isn't going to be easy.*

He started with a historical perspective—how the mother world devised an ingenious method to colonize the stars and get rid of all its malcontents, dissidents, and troublemakers in a single stroke: a promise of one-way passage to an Earth-type planet to any group of sufficient size that wanted to set up the utopia of its choice. It became known as the era of the splinter worlds, and there was no shortage of takers. Soon most of the habitable worlds in a sphere around Earth were peopled with all sorts of oddball societies, most of which collapsed within a few years of landfall.

The Shaper colony was an exception. Its pioneers were all well-grounded in science and technology and managed to build a viable society. Their goal was a world of physically perfect human telepaths and they were well on their way when the Teratol clique took over. That was when teries were formed; that was when the Hole was started; and finally, that was when the virus that caused the Great Sickness—the pandemic holocaust—was born.

A small group of the surviving Shapers banded together during the plague. They saw their civilization coming apart and wanted something preserved, so they gathered samples of all the available technology of their time into one spot and sealed it up. They then wrote a brief history of the colony in five volumes and buried it for posterity. Before they, too, succumbed to the Great Sickness, they beamed the contents of the volumes into space.

The message was received. But this was in the days of the beleaguered outworld Imperium, which had little interest in rescuing diseased Shapers. So the message was dutifully recorded and forgotten. It was only after the LaNague Federation rose from the ruins of the Imperium, and the Cultural Survey teams were started in an attempt to bring surviving splinter worlds back into the mainstream of humanity, that the transcript of the five-volume transmission was found.

Steven Dalt, fresh from his infiltration of the feudal splinter culture of Kwashi, was given the job.

"Are you following me so far?" Dalt asked.

The tery neither shook his head nor nodded. "What is a planet?" he asked.

"What's a pla—?"

Dalt then realized that for all its native intelligence, Jon's mind was primitively unsophisticated in its ability to grasp cosmological concepts. The stars were points of light, the planet on which they stood was "the world" and the primary it circled, "the sun." This talk about the LaNague Federation and splinter worlds and interstellar colonization had been totally incomprehensible to the

tery—like discussing the big bang theory with someone who still believed in a geocentric universe.
Yet Jon had listened patiently and with interest,
whether through personal regard for Dalt or through
a desire to have someone—anyone—address him
as a fellow rational being, Dalt could not say.

"Let's put off that explanation for some other
time, Jon, and just accept the fact that I was sent
from a faraway land to see how things were going
here."

Things were not going well at all, as he had soon
discovered after landing and camouflaging his craft.
A preliminary survey had located the population
centers, made language recordings, and returned
to Fed Central. Dalt absorbed the language—a
pidgin version of Old Earth Anglic—via encephalo-
augmentation and was readied to pose as one of
the natives to assess their suitability to handle
modern technology. Since they favored hard con-
sonants in their male names, he turned his own
around. And since he did not want too close contact with the locals, he posed as a reclusive potter
deep in the forests.

His advent coincided with Mekk's order for extermination of the Talents and he found himself
acting as potter and confidant to a unique group of
telepaths. Here was something every Cultural Survey operative dreamed of finding: A group of humans split off from the mainstream of the race,
developing a separate and distinct life style. This
was the very purpose for which the CSS had been
formed.

But on this planet they were marked for extinction.

So Dalt had sent an urgent request by subspace laser for an intervention by the Federation Defense Force to protect these psis and let them follow their course. And had been turned down.

"It's up to you and me, my furry friend," he told Jon, the tery. "I'll get no help from my friends back in my homeland" —*and I can't even use a blaster, though I'll be damned if I won't carry one with me when we go to the Hole*—"so we're going to have to carry the show. Let's go see Rab."

"Here's an entry port to the observation corridor," Dalt said, pointing to a small, dark blot on the map. Then he sketched an arc with his finger. "And here's the perimeter of the routine patrols around Mekk's fortress."

The blot fell between the arc and the fortress.

"We can sneak past the patrols," Rab said.

"We need to do more than sneak. We're going to have to dig our way in. The port is buried."

Rab frowned. "That's a problem. They'll catch us sure."

"That's where your people come in. Can we count on them?"

"Of course. What do you need?"

"A war."

"Now wait just a—"

"A small war," Dalt said with a smile. "One played by *our* rules."

The Talents moved their camp deeper into the forest, putting more distance between themselves and Mekk's fortress. Then the archers moved forward and ringed the fortress in small groups.

The war began.

The Talents developed into a perfectly coordinated guerrilla force, striking then disappearing like fish in the sea. When Mekk's generals sent a hundred men out to search the surrounding trees, they found nothing. When they sent ten men out to investigate a minor disturbance, none came back.

The net result of these seemingly random skirmishes was a gradual withdrawal of the patrol lines toward the fortress, a tightening of the perimeters, just as Dalt had intended. This gave him, Rab, and Jon, the tery, a chance to locate the old entry port to the corridor that ran parallel to the Hole. Working all night and well into the next day, as swiftly and silently as they could, they moved rocks and dug through the dirt until they had made an opening just big enough for the tery to slip through.

Dalt nodded to Rab as he prepared to follow Jon. Rab was to wait by the entrance and use his Talent to summon help if necessary. He squeezed through the opening—

And entered the anteroom to Hell.

Dalt had been expecting the worst, but nothing hinted at in his transcript of the Shaper history had prepared him for the sights that greeted him.

The forgotten corridor stretched before them with a gentle curve to the left. The left wall was composed of a thick transparent substance that jutted out into the Hole at a forty-five degree angle. Its far surface was smeared with a mixture of dried blood, excrement, and dirt, undoubtedly left there by generations of Hole inhabitants trying to claw their way out.

But there was no way out. The rock that made up the floor, sides, and ceiling of the Hole had been treated by the Teratol clique to make it impervious to any digging or tunneling attempts. The only access to the outside world was through the vertical shafts leading to the ventilation grates, and these were lined with the same impenetrable glassy substance that now separated Dalt and Jon from the Hole.

The porous rock that lined the inner surface of the Hole had been treated in another way: it glowed. The light arose from all sides, totally eliminating shadow, creating an endless twilight that added to the surreal, nightmarish quality of the hellish panorama before them.

For food, the Teratols had developed a rapidly growing fungus that hung from the ceiling of the Hole in stalagtitic abundance. For water there were a number of underground springs that fed into a large pool at the center of the cavern. The temperature was a damp, cool, subterranean constant. For those who required shelter, a hidey-hole could be dug into the porous rock that had not been treated against it. There was no wood, there was no fire, there were no tools of any sort.

None of the Teratol mistakes would ever escape, none would ever starve, none would ever die of thirst, none would ever freeze.

And none would ever know a moment's peace.

There was no social order in the Hole. The strongest, the fiercest, the ones that hunted best in packs—these ruled the Hole. The weak, the timid, the sick, the lame became either food or slaves. The sense of entrapment, plus the foul living conditions, compounded by generations of inbreeding, had reduced the inhabitants of the Hole to a horde of savage, imbecilic monstrosities.

"This is the darkest side of the human soul, Jon," Dalt said. "Anything that's good and decent within us has been banished from here."

With Jon gliding behind him, Dalt walked along the corridor, queasily watching as scenes of nightmarish barbarism that were a part of day-to-day existence in the Hole played out before him.

A creature with an amorphous body, six tentacles, and a humanoid head shuffled along, picking up morsels of fungus and stuffing them into its mouth. Without warning, another creature, reptilian in body with horny plates projecting from its back—and again, the humanoid head, always a humanoid head—launched itself from a burrow about a meter off the floor and landed on the tentacled creature's back. With sharp fangs it tore into the flesh of its victim's neck until blood spouted over both of them. The victim rolled onto its side, however, and managed to wrap one of its longer tentacles around the attacker's throat.

Dalt could not bear to wait and see whether the first's blood supply could outlast the other's oxygen. He left the combatants writhing on the other side of the window and pressed on, trying not to watch the endless variety of depraved forms that skulked, leaped, crawled, shuttled, scuttled, and ran through the small area of the Hole that was visible to them. Yet he was unable to turn completely away.

"There's a door somewhere along here," he told Jon. "The Teratols made one entry from the corridor into the Hole. I just hope we can open it when we find it."

The tery said nothing and Dalt glanced at his companion, wondering if he could hold his own in there. Jon would have two advantages—his intelligence and his hunting club. Dalt had wanted to give him a blaster, but the tery had been too frightened of its power. He seemed more comfortable with the weapon that had protected him and helped feed him for most of his life. So a club it was.

I wouldn't go in there with two *blasters*, Dalt thought, glancing into the Hole again.

He estimated from the difference in light levels between the cavern and the corridor that the dwellers on the other side of the window probably didn't even know the corridor existed. The light from the phosphorescent stone would reflect off the filth smeared on the window, making it look like an unusually smooth section of the wall. The Shapers had probably wanted it that way so they could watch without being seen.

Jon stopped abruptly and pointed to something on the window.

"What is that, Tlad?"

Dalt saw a round, dark splotch, about the length of a man's arm in diameter, edging its way down the Hole side of the window. He tried to get a peek at what it looked like on the reverse but it must have been flat and disk-shaped. He could make out no protrusions from the other side.

A movement to the right caught his eye. Down a narrow path came five dark shapes, low to the ground, scuttling. The disk must have had an eye on the other side, too; must have seen the approaching shapes, for it reversed direction.

Then the shapes were close enough for Dalt to make out details: They had normal human heads and torsos, but all resemblance to humanity as Dalt knew it ended there. Each had dark skin and eight legs—four to a side—which were articulated spider-style. But it was the naked hunger-fury in their blank, idiotic faces as they swarmed up to the window and attacked the disk that made Dalt leap backwards and slam against the far wall of the corridor. The movement was involuntary. Intellectually, he knew he was safe. Emotionally . . . that was another matter.

Then came a further horror. After the spider gang had peeled the disk from the wall and was carrying it away to wherever it was they lived, Dalt saw its other side. There were only a few details, but even in the dim light a fleeting glance showed beyond a doubt the features of a human face.

Jon's eyes snapped to him. He had seen it, too.

"This is how they must live?" he asked Dalt. "Why was this done to them? Why must this be?"

Dalt arched himself away from the the wall and came over to the tery. He had developed a genuine affection for this innocent in beast's clothing. Jon could not comprehend the corruption of spirit that could occur when one human found he had absolute control over the existence of another. Neither could Dalt, but he knew more of human history than the tery.

"Jon, my friend," he said, putting his hand on the tery's shoulder as they began walking again, "none of this *must* be. This is a hideous fabrication, a product of the worst in us. It doesn't *have* to be, but it is. Nothing that can happen to us by chance is anywhere near as awful as what we somehow manage to do to each other by design."

" 'We?' " Jon said. "Who is 'we?' I would never do this!"

"I was speaking of all humanity in general—and that includes you, my friend, like it or not."

"But I am not a 'we' for this," Jon rumbled in his deep voice. "I would like to be a 'we' with you and Rab and Komak and Adriel, but no . . . I am not a 'we' in this. Never!"

The note of finality in Jon's voice made Dalt decide not to pursue the matter any further. They walked in silence.

The door was unmistakable when they came upon it. The windowed wall of the corridor had been one long, uninterrupted, seamless transparency. After following the curving passage along an arc of approximately forty degrees, they saw the window terminate at what appeared to be a huge steel column, perhaps three meters across, reaching from floor to ceiling. The window continued its course on the far side of the column.

"This has to be it," Dalt said as he inspected the smooth metallic surface.

He found a recess large enough to admit four fingers; he inserted them and pulled. Nothing. He scanned the door again and found three small disks at eye level.

"The code—I forgot!"

He reached into a pouch in his belt and pulled

out a slip of paper. The combination was *Clear*,
1-3-1-3-2-3-1-2.

"Clear? How do you clear?"

The transcript had never said. It gave the combination sequence, but never explained how to
clear the circuit.

Playing a hunch, Dalt pressed all three disks at
once and was rewarded by a soft glow within each.
He tapped in the sequence. When he put his
fingers into the notch and pulled this time, a panel
swung out on silent hinges, revealing a small chamber. The ceiling began to glow as they stepped
inside.

Before them was another door, a narrow one,
secured by four steel bars, each as thick around as
a man's thigh. Dalt noticed a wheel on the wall to
his left and began to turn it. The bars moved. The
first and third bars began to withdraw to the right,
the second and fourth to the left.

Dalt stopped turning when the bars had moved
half their distance.

"All right," he said. "We know we can get in.
Do we want to?"

Jon cocked his head questioningly.

"I mean," Dalt said, "can you make it? Is there
really a decent chance of your getting to the cache
and back again through that . . . that nightmare in
there?"

He was having second thoughts about this whole
affair. He had never thought it would be easy, but
the Hole had turned out to be a more awesome
obstacle then he had ever imagined. So he was
offering the tery a way out, and hoping he'd take
it.

For despite all Jon's strength and cunning, Dalt seriously doubted he could last very long in there.

"I *must* go."

"No, you mustn't *anything*! You . . ." He paused briefly as his throat tightened. "I don't want you to die, Jon."

He meant it. There was something in this misshapen young man that he wanted to preserve and keep nearby. He didn't know whether to label it innocence or nobility or a combination of both. But it was good and it was alive and he didn't want to see it torn to pieces in the Hole.

Jon tried to smile—it was a practiced grimace that did not come naturally to his face.

"I will not die."

"You may. You may very well die in there. So think hard before deciding."

"There is nothing to decide, Tlad. I am the only one who can go. A human—I mean, one who looks like a human—cannot go. Only a tery has a chance of sneaking through. So I must go. There is no one else."

"No! We can find another way. Mekk won't be able to get through there, either. He'll never reach the cache. The Talents can hide in the forests and grow and maybe wait this out. You don't have to die for them!"

"I will not die. I will save them, and then they will have to recognize me as a human. They will have to accord me the honor of thinking of me as a man."

So that's it, Dalt thought.

This was Jon the tery's trial by combat into the human race.

"That's not necessary, Jon. You—"

"I am going, Tlad." Again, that note of finality. "Tell me what to find."

"If you go at all, you're going to have to go twice!" Dalt said, then waited for the expected effect.

Jon remained impassive. "Then I shall go twice. But tell me why. I was to find the cache and bring back sufficient weapons for the Talents to—"

"There will be no weapons for the Talents," Dalt said. "I fear the weapons will harm the psi-folk as much as they'll help them. The arms in the cache will give them too much power; they may even lead to the rise of another type of Mekk . . . a worse type . . . one with the Talent."

A nightmare scenario had been running through his brain. He saw the Talents rising up with their new-found energy weapons and overthrowing Mekk; he saw them executing Mekk's troopers and the True Shape priests. All well and good, all to be expected. But then he saw them eliminating all followers of the True Shape religion, as well as all supporters of the Extermination Decree. And after that, all those who hadn't actively *opposed* the decree. And on and on until only Talents remained.

"You do not trust Rab?" Jon said.

"Rab is a good man. But I don't know if his character—or anybody else's—can withstand the corrosive effect of absolute power. And even if he proves to be a match for it, he will not be the only leader the Talents ever have. The cache must be destroyed."

Jon made no comment; he merely locked his eyes with Dalt's.

"Do you trust *me*?" Dalt asked finally.

"I'd be dead if not for you."

"That doesn't mean I'm right and that doesn't mean you should trust me. It only means I—"

"I trust you!" Jon said softly, his voice echoing in the tiny chamber.

"Good," Dalt said in a low voice. "Because I trust you, too. I believe in you."

In the dust on the floor of the chamber he drew a picture of the explosive device he wanted Jon to procure from the cache. It was ovoid in shape, small enough to fit comfortably in the tery's hand, and powerful enough to set off a chain reaction among the other weapons stored there. From the inventory described in Dalt's transcript, there was enough explosive power available in the cache to make a shambles of Mekk's fortress above, permanently ending his petty empire of fear.

The device had a timer that could only be set by hand—it had no capacity for detonation by remote control, unfortunately—and the procedure was too complex for someone who had never handled a timer before. That was why the tery would have to make two trips: the first to bring it back to Dalt for the time-setting; the second to return it to the cache.

"And the Hole dwellers? What happens to them?" Jon asked.

"This entire cavern will collapse. Their misery will be over, along with Mekk's rule."

The tery considered this in silence.

"I think that's for the best," Dalt said. "Don't you?"

"Can we decide this for them?"

The question rattled Dalt for a moment. He had not expected his ethics to be questioned by a forest-dwelling savage like Jon. But then, why not? Jon killed, but only in defense or out of hunger. And he killed one to one, looking his victims in the eyes. Why wouldn't he question the killing of thousands of creatures who were locked away and posed no threat to him?

Why didn't I question it? Dalt thought, uneasily.

"Jon, if you can see another way, tell me."

"I trust you, Tlad."

That seemed to be enough for Jon, but those four words were dead weight on Dalt's shoulders.

Dalt then showed him how to work the combination studs. There would be a set on the door to the cache identical to those here. He drilled him until he had the sequence firmly committed to memory.

"That's all I can do for you," Dalt said after a final run-through of the description of the device and the combination. "A door identical to this outer one here is imbedded in a wall of rock adjacent to the central pool. Head straight out from here and you should find it. And keep moving!"

He turned the wheel until the bars on the inner door were fully retracted, then ran out to the window to make sure all was clear. Returning to the chamber, he grasped Jon's huge right hand in his own.

"Good luck, brother."

Jon growled something unintelligible, then together they pulled the door open. Dank, sour, fetid air poured over them as the tery leaped through and began to run. Dalt pushed the door closed and turned the wheel until the bars just overlapped the edge of the door—just enough to keep some Hole dweller from lumbering through by accident, but not enough to cause any significant delay when Jon returned.

Then he went to the window and watched. And waited.

XIII

The stench.

He hadn't been prepared for the stench.

It struck him like a blow. The odors of rotting flesh, stale urine, and fresh feces assaulted his acutely perceptive olfactory senses as soon as the door opened. But above all was the unmistakable scent of kill-or-be-killed tension. It saturated the air, permeated the walls.

He moved straight out from the door and entered a winding passage that curved left, then right. The palm of his right hand was sweaty where it gripped his hunting club.

Jon was frightened. He had disguised his fear when talking to Tlad—had almost hidden it from himself, then—but now it came screaming to the surface. He was trembling, ready to strike out at or jump away from anything that moved or came near him.

This was not the forest. The rules here were all

different, as unique as they were deadly. The softly glowing rock walls on either side of him were pocked from floor to ceiling with burrows and recesses. Any mad, frenzied creature of any shape, imaginable or otherwise, could be lurking within, ready to pounce, ready to maim or kill without provocation.

He maintained his pace at a wary trot, first upright, then bent, using his left arm as an extra leg, eyes continually moving left, right, above, and behind. So far, no sign of Hole dwellers. There were dark things pulled back tight into the burrows around him, he knew—things that might rush and leap upon him were he smaller and less sure-footed.

The passage widened ahead and forked left and right. His innate sense of direction led him to the right, but as he started down the new path, he heard a cacophony of scraping feet, growls of rage and grunts of pain from around the bend not far ahead of him. And it was moving closer.

Looking up, he spotted a ledge within reach above his head. He pulled himself up and lay flat on his belly with only his eyes and his forehead exposed. The noises grew louder, and then the source staggered around the bend in the passage.

At first he thought it was a huge, dark, nodular creature with multiple human heads and uncountable black spindly arms waving frantically in all directions. But as it moved closer, Jon realized that it was a gang of the spiderlike teries he and Tlad had seen earlier—perhaps the same gang, perhaps a new one—attacking another larger creature en masse.

The lone victim suddenly reared up on its hind legs and threw off four or five of its attackers, but an equal number remained attached. Jon saw that this creature was taller than he, and vaguely human in form, although grotesquely out of proportion. Its round, bald head was affixed to its body without benefit of a neck; its shoulders were massive, as were its arms which reached nearly to the ground when it raised itself erect. From the shoulders the body tapered sharply to a narrow pelvis and ludicrously short, stubby legs.

Jon also saw what the spider gang was after: not the creature itself, but the three small wriggling children clinging to its underbelly. That and its four flattened breasts labeled it a female.

And a female to be reckoned with! Her hugely muscled arms swatted fiercely at the members of the spider gang, keeping them away from her young as she struggled to reach shelter. She was holding her own until two of the spider-men attached themselves to her shoulders and started clawing at her eyes.

This last happened as the group passed below Jon's perch. He knew it would be much to his advantage to let them all move on by and finish their battle further down the passage. But something in that misshapen mother's fierce, selfless defense of her equally misshapen brood touched him. He had to intervene.

Just this once, he promised himself.

He leaned over the edge of the ledge and swung his club at the nearest spider-man on her back, putting all of his arm and a good deal of his back behind the blow. The club cracked across the mid-

dle of the creature's spine and it went spinning to
the floor where it lay screeching incoherently and
kicking—but only the two forward legs were kicking. The second spider-thing looked up at Jon with
unfocused fury in the imbecilic eyes of its human
face, then launched itself upward with a howl.
There was no revenge motive in its action, only
hunger at the sight of what appeared to be a
vulnerable prey.

The howl caught the attention of the other gang
members and for an instant they withdrew from
their attack on the mother and her young. She did
not hesitate to take advantage of it: a huge arm
lashed out and grabbed one of the spider-things by
two of its legs, then lifted it and smashed it against
the floor again and again until the two limbs were
torn free of their sockets and the rest of the pulpy
body skidded across the floor to land against a wall
and lay still.

Jon stopped watching to deal with the second
spider-thing. Its leap had brought it to the ledge
and from there it lunged directly at Jon's face. He
battered at it before it could reach him. Four wild
bone-breaking swings of his club and the creature
was knocked from the ledge. The rest of the gang
looked on its three fallen members and fled back
the way they had come.

The mother went over to the creature with the
injured spine and halted its screeching with two
crushing blows to the head. She then checked the
body of the one that had fallen from the ledge.
Satisfied that none would ever bother her again,
she backed up to where she could get a look at
Jon.

Standing erect, she stared at him, as if her dull mind were trying to comprehend why he had helped her. Jon wasn't so sure himself, and now wondered if it had been a foolish gesture. She had him trapped here on this ledge and could easily reach up with those long arms and grab him.

They watched each other.

She still clutched the two legs she had ripped from one of the spider-things. The three little monstrosities clinging to her abdomen began to wriggle and squeal. Without taking her eyes from Jon, she put the bloody end of one of the legs up to her wide mouth and nibbled off a piece of raw flesh. She chewed rapidly without swallowing, then took small bits of the masticated meat from her mouth and fed them to her young. With an abrupt motion, she stepped closer to Jon's ledge and held up the untasted leg to him.

Suppressing a retch, he leaped to the ground and fled down the passage.

These were once human? he asked himself when his stomach had settled and he had slowed from a run to a jog. *Or are they still human despite what they've become?*

And where does Jon the tery fit in?

No answers came.

He arrived at the central pool, a stagnant body of water fed by a slow underground spring. Something on the far side lapped briefly at the pristine smoothness of the water's surface, then scuttled away.

It was dark in this region. Perhaps the excess moisture had a deteriorative effect on the phos-

phorescence. Whatever the cause, it made finding
the door Tlad had described more difficult.

Jon began scouting the water's edge, looking for
a rock wall with a door in it. He found it almost by
accident—if he had not been dragging his left
hand against the rock as he searched, he would
have passed without noticing it. But his fingers felt
a long vertical groove and he stopped to inspect.

The notched handle was there. So were the
three studs.

Water rippled behind him. He turned and saw
nothing at first other than a bubbling disturbance
at the center of the otherwise flawless surface.
Another ripple and he spotted something floating
on—no, rising from the pool. He could not make
out the shape and did not care to. Whatever it
was, it did not wish him well—not here in the
Hole.

Brushing off the studs, he quickly tapped in the
code: 1-3-1-3-2-3-1-2, then grabbed for the notch.
The door stayed firm. He tried the code again and
still no result.

A glance over his shoulder showed him that
something monstrously huge had risen from the
pool and was looming over him. He tried the
sequence again but the door wouldn't budge! He
was frantically beating his fist against it when Tlad's
words came back to him:

"Whatever you do, don't forget to clear."

Jon hit all three buttons at once, tapped in the
sequence, and pulled. It moved! Dust, dirt, and
pebbles powdered him as he dropped his club,
thrust both hands into the notch, placed his left
foot against the wall, and pulled with desperate

strength. He didn't have to look behind now—moist
air from the formless behemoth's cold wet surface
was wafting around him as it reared over him.

The door suddenly jerked open and he fell back
against something cold and soft and slimy, then he
catapulted himself into the opening, pulling the
door behind him. It closed only halfway. Fallen
debris was jamming it open. The creature outside,
however, solved the problem for him by lumbering against the door and forcing it closed with his
weight.

The room seemed to sense Jon's presence. Pan-
els in the ceiling began to glow, adding to the
luminescence in the walls. Jon tried to gather his
wits. The room was loaded with crates: they lined
the walls and stood in long rows before him. Where
to begin?

After a brief rest—this was the first time since
leaving Tlad that he felt safe enough to let down
his guard—he started with the pile on his left and
moved along the wall, tearing open the flimsy
packing of the crates with his hands. Some held
books, others drawings and pictures, but most of
the contents were totally incomprehensible to him.
More things he didn't understand.

So many things he didn't understand!

Tlad was one. Why did he trust that man? He
had already lied to everyone a number of times.
Tlad wasn't his real name . . . he did not come
from the coast . . . he was not a potter.

Why trust a liar?

Tlad had spent days talking to Jon, trying to
explain where he came from and why he was here.
All Jon could glean from the monologues was that

he came from far away and wanted to help the
Talents and all other teries.

Why? Did he have reasons he wasn't telling?
Had he lied to Jon about his intentions as he had
lied about his name?

But Tlad had *talked* to Jon, treated him as a
man, truly seemed to think of him as one. Because
of that, Jon would do almost anything for Tlad . . .
even aid him in deceiving Rab and the Talents by
destroying the weapons instead of bringing them
back. Tlad said it was for the best and Jon believed
him.

He found the bombs eventually. Crates of them,
all neatly stacked against the wall. They were egg-
shaped as Tlad had said, with a smooth, shiny
surface.

These could kill? These could destroy the Hole
and Mekk's fortress as well? It did not seem possible. But he had trusted Tlad this far . . .

Only one was needed. He cupped this in the
palm of his hand and returned to the door. Pressing his ear against its smooth metal surface, he
listened for signs of activity outside. All was quiet.
The door moved easily at his touch and he stepped
back as it swung outward. Nothing but the narrow
path and a smooth expanse of water awaited him.

The inhabitant of the lake was gone.

The lights in the cache room dimmed slowly as
he exited and were fully extinguished by the time
the door clicked shut behind him. He looked down
and saw his club where he had dropped it. It was
covered with slime—everything was covered with
slime. Wiping the handle of the weapon clean
against the fur on his leg, he followed the slime

trail along the edge of the pool and noted that it wandered off into the passage he had planned on taking back to Tlad.

He changed his plans. Despite the fact that the path in question was the one that brought him here and was the only one he knew, and despite the fact that his greatest fear in the Hole was to become lost, he decided to take another route.

He would trust his sense of direction on a strange path more than he would trust his club against the dark behemoth from the pool.

The new passage was not very much different from the other and he made good time, loping along on his hind legs with the bomb cradled in his left hand against his chest, his club swinging back and forth in his right.

Then trouble.

Rounding a bend in the passage, he literally ran into a pack of nine or ten spider-things.

Without the slightest hesitation, they were on him with howls of fury, their clawed arms raking at him, their sharp teeth in their all-too-human faces snapping at him. Jon shook them off and backed up slowly, swinging his club sparingly but with telling effect, always keeping it menacingly before him.

After the initial assault, the gang kept its distance, constantly trying to flank him, or work one of its members behind him. Jon kept backpedalling, holding them before him, wondering how long he could keep this up.

Suddenly there was stone against his back and nowhere to go. He had allowed them to corral him into a dead-end branch of the passage. His gut writhed with fear as he glanced around. They had him boxed in. He was trapped.

He looked up and saw the dark mouth of a small cave just out of reach above him. He could climb there easily, but it would mean turning his back on the gang of spider-things, and he didn't dare do that.

Just then they attacked in earnest—a suicide charge on three levels with some leaping for his legs, others for his arms, and others for his head. Whirling and swinging his club, kicking when opportunity presented, Jon managed to hold them off for a moment or two, then one of them sank its teeth into his leg. Jon twisted and lost his balance. He went down on one knee. As the gang swarmed over him, their teeth and claws tearing at him, their loathsome black bodies rubbing against him, Jon felt himself start to fall onto his back. He dropped his club and raised his right arm for balance, searching for support, anything to keep him upright. For if they got him down on the ground—

Suddenly he felt powerful fingers close about his wrist. With a force that threatened to pull his arm from its socket, he was lifted partly free of his attackers. He kicked them off as he was hauled into the air and unceremoniously dumped into the cave above. He whirled, ready to face a threat worse than that below, and was startled to see the mother monster he had aided earlier.

She hissed and pushed him behind her, then returned her attention to the furious spider gang below. As they swarmed up the wall, she sat back and waited. As soon as one would poke its head inside the cave mouth, she would punch at it with one of her huge fists. Her arms worked like battering rams. She seemed to be enjoying herself.

Jon would have helped her but he had lost his club. He was relieved to see that he still had the egg-shaped bomb. He looked around for something else to use against the attackers but found nothing. He did come across the corpse of one of the spider-things slain earlier. The mother's young were clustered around it, nibbling.

Toward the rear of the cave, Jon noticed a shaft of light. Curious, he stepped over the younglings' grisly feast and went to investigate. The tunnel curved sharply upward but the light ahead was an irresistible lure. He climbed swiftly.

There was a break slightly smaller than his head in the back wall of the cave. Light poured through it—not the sickly phosphorescent glow that permeated the Hole, but a brighter, cleaner, familiar light.

Sunlight.

Jon put his face to the opening and looked through. He found he was looking into a large vertical shaft with sheer, smooth, unblemished walls. From above where the sunlight filtered down, a gong was clanging and a man began screaming. By leaning his shoulder against the wall, he found he could twist his neck and see to the top of the shaft. A heavy iron grate covered the opening. Above that was blue sky and a ring of humans.

The grate was lifted and a naked, struggling, terrified man was brought to the edge. His arms were tied behind him; his screaming had stopped, reduced now to pitiful whimpering. A voice was speaking in measured tones, the words indistinct, perhaps praying, perhaps reading a sentence . . .

Something unsettlingly familiar about that voice . . .

When the voice stopped, the man began screaming again. The two troopers holding him gave a powerful shove and he fell free with wildly flailing legs and a cry of utter despair and terror that followed him all the way down the shaft, ending abruptly in a chorus of growls and scuffles from the waiting Hole dwellers below. Jon could not see the floor of the shaft. He did not want to.

He watched instead the vulpine faces of the troopers above him as they squinted into the dimness below, trying to catch some of the more grisly details of their ex-prisoner's fate. Then another face joined them in peering over the edge and Jon felt his hackles rise.

He knew this man! Ghentren, the captain from Kitru's keep!

Suddenly, it was all back—all the grief, the anguish, the rage, the pain. Not that any of them had really faded away, but somehow his close association with Tlad and the Talents had eased them to the back of his mind, layered them over with a soothing salve, and hidden them under clean dressings. He had thought he was healing, but knew now that nothing had healed. The heat from those festering, supperating wounds was more intense than ever.

He could hear his teeth grinding of their own accord. He wanted Captain Ghentren's blood as much as ever. The balance craved restoration . . .

. . . and would have it!

Jon pulled back from the opening and pondered the situation. He could not get to Ghentren on his own. He would need Tlad's help. He looked at the death egg in his hand and knew it was the key. The bomb would assure Tlad's cooperation. He hefted it in his left hand and began to slide down the incline toward the mouth of the tunnel.

The mother creature awaited him with her brood clustered about her. The spider gang was gone—either driven off or finally and forcefully convinced of the futility of trying to gain entrance to the cave. She pressed back against the wall to let him pass and hissed as he did so.

Jon kept his distance and tensed when he saw her reach for something on the floor. But she was only picking up one of the dead spider-thing's legs. She offered it to him once more.

Jon steeled himself and took it from her.

She bared her teeth at him. If it was a smile, it was a poor attempt at one. But in her eyes, he thought he detected a sadness that he had to go. Perhaps loneliness was the greatest horror in the Hole.

Jon waved and quickly made his exit, leaving her alone in her little cave with her brood. As he climbed down the wall toward the floor, he realized that if, as Tlad had said, the Shapers had intended the Hole to be peopled by creatures from whom every shred of human decency had been removed, they had failed: At least so far as the mother creature was concerned, a favor had not been forgotten, nor allowed to go unrepaid. Amid all this depravity, a spark of fellowship could still glow.

Reaching the floor, Jon paused to get his bearings and noticed two dead spider gang members at the foot of the wall. His club lay between them, untouched—he guessed the hands of the spiderthings were not built to wield such a weapon. He retrieved it, then made his way out of the cul-desac and back down the passage toward the doorway to the observation corridor and safety.

When he had almost reached his destination, Jon halted and searched the softly glowing dirt and rock that lined the walls on either side of him. He located a loose stone at eye level and pried it out. After scraping out a small hollow, he placed the bomb within and pressed the stone back over it, then stepped back and surveyed his work. Satisfied with the job of concealment, he turned and ran the rest of the way back to Tlad.

XIV

"He made it!" Dalt shouted to the empty corridor when he saw Jon's familiar form break from a pile of stony rubble and race toward him.

He jumped back from the window and dashed into the lock. Grabbing the wheel on the wall, he spun it until the locking bars slid free of the door, then pulled it open. Jon leaped through and helped him close it after him.

"Thank the Core you're all right!" he said.

It was all he could do to keep from hugging this big, bearish youth. All the while Jon had been gone, Dalt had imagined a thousand gruesome deaths and had sworn never to forgive himself if anything happened to him in there.

But now it was over and the tery didn't look any worse for the wear—no, wait a minute—there was blood on his face, neck, and back . . .

"You're hurt?"

"Just scratches," Jon said in his growly voice.

161

He was breathing easily, evenly as he stood there. "Only hurt a little."

"Did you find the cache?"

"Yes. Found it. Found the bombs—many of them." There was an odd tenseness about him as he spoke.

"Well . . . where is it?"

An instant of hesitation. "Out there."

"You dropped it?"

"I hid it."

Dalt was baffled. "Explain, Jon."

The tery quickly recounted what and whom he had seen in the air shaft. He concluded by telling Dalt what he now desired most in life.

"Captain Ghentren must die."

"Oh, he'll die all right," Dalt assured him. "Everyone up there—Mekk, the priests, the troopers—they'll all go when that one bomb sets off the others."

"No. You do not understand. He must not die without knowing. He must realize that his death restores a balance that he upset when he came to my home and killed my parents. He must *know* that before he dies!"

"It's called vengeance, Jon," Dalt said slowly. "And you've certainly got some coming—generations' worth. But the bombs will provide it with interest."

"No," the tery repeated. "You do not understand. That captain must—"

"He must squirm and plead and beg before you kill him? Is that what you mean? Is that what you want? You want to sink to the level of his tactics, is that it?"

Struck by the vehemence of Dalt's voice, Jon stiffened but made no reply.

"You're better than that, Jon! Rab told me how you killed Dennel and Kitru, but that was different—that was when you were trapped in the middle of hostile territory."

"Yes. And because of men like the captain, the whole world is hostile territory to my kind!"

"That may be, but what you're talking about now is not like you. It's cold-blooded and not worthy of you." His voice softened. "You may not know it, Jon, but there's something noble and good and decent about you. People sense it. That's why they like you. This Captain Ghentren is scum, no better and no worse than the others up there who do Mekk's bidding. Don't dirty your hands on him!"

"But the balance—"

"Blast the balance! The bombs will take care of that!"

"*No!*" the note of irrevocable finality in the tery's voice brought Dalt's arguments to an abrupt halt. "The bomb will not be replaced in the cache until I have seen the parent-slayer's blood on my hands!"

"And now blackmail," Dalt said in a low whisper. "You learn fast, don't you?"

He ached inside as he faced Jon. The poor fellow had been through so much in such a short time. His home, his security, his very identity had been shattered. His world had begun to spin wildly out of control when Ghentren's men spilled his parents' blood, and something within him clung desperately to the belief that all would be set on an even keel again by the death of this same Captain Ghentren.

"What do you want me to do?" Dalt asked, dully watching innocence crumble before him.

"Find Ghentren," the tery rasped. "There is still daylight left and you can go above in the fortress and find out where he sleeps."

"And then what?"

"I will visit him tonight and restore the balance."

"You can't even get into the fortress, let alone kill an officer!"

"I can. And I will. Then I will return and replace the death egg after you have done what you must do to it."

Dalt considered his options and found he had none. He was bound by the Cultural Survey Service regulations to work within the technological stratum of the society under observation, but that wasn't holding him back now. It was the Hole. It stood between him and the solution to this mess. He stared through the window at the eternal nightmare. If he thought he had the slightest chance of surviving in there, he'd go himself. But only a full Defense Force combat rig would get him through the Hole alive, and he hadn't brought one along.

He could abort the entire mission. But if he did that, it was tantamount to handing all those weapons directly over to Mekk, for sooner or later the Overlord would find a way to get to them. And that would be the end of the Talents and anything else that dared to deviate from what the True Shape sect decided was the norm on this world.

Damn the Fed and damn the CS Service! Why couldn't they establish a protectorate?

He was getting tired of asking himself that question and receiving no answers . . . no answers he liked.

"Since I have no choice," he told Jon, "and since the future well-being of our friends, the Talents, depends on placing that bomb"—he glared at the tery but saw that Jon remained unmoved—"I'll do what I can. But I'll need your help to get to the surface."

Jon said nothing but stood quietly, waiting for Dalt to get started.

Feeling at once saddened and exhausted, Dalt spun the wheel that locked the door into the Hole and turned away. The diagrams in his transcript of Shaper history had shown one or two air shafts leading up from the observation corridor, as they did from the Hole. These, however, were equipped with ladders. They found one further on down the passage. Dalt climbed up the imbedded rungs and peered through the grate set in the wall of the shaft like a window.

The opening appeared to be situated in the side wall of a two-meter pipe, part of the original city's drainage system. A lever on his right unlatched the grate and it swung open easily. With Jon close behind, he eased himself through and scuttled around the puddles to where a faint shaft of sunlight cut the gloom at a sharp angle.

Another grate, this one in the roof of the pipe. He clung to its underside and saw that it opened into the floor of an alley. Shadows were lengthening and all seemed quiet. He sensed no one about. Moving his hand along the edge of the grate, he found what he wanted: a lever, rusty with disuse.

After applying most of his weight to it, there came
a creak of metal on metal and the lever moved,
releasing the grate.

Moving that was another matter, however. The
full force of the muscles in his back and legs was
not enough to budge the heavy iron structure. The
combination of ponderous weight and rusty hinges
was proof against his strongest efforts.

But not against Jon's. The tery glided up beside
him and threw his shoulder against the grate. With
an agonized whine of protest, it swung upward
until there was enough of an opening for Dalt to
squeeze through. The tery eased it shut as soon as
he was clear.

A quick glance around showed Dalt that his
initial assessment had been correct: he was in a
deserted alley. He peered down through the grate
and saw Jon's face hovering in the darkness on the
other side.

"Wait here," he told the tery. "Get ready to
open this thing as soon as you see me. I don't
know what I'm going to find up here and I may
want to get back down there in a big hurry."

"I will wait," was Jon's only reply.

Dalt walked slowly to where the alley merged
with a narrow thoroughfare and looked about. There
was little traffic this time of day. The civilians from
the village down the hill had sold their wares or
done their assigned tasks and were gradually filter-
ing out of the fortress and returning to their homes.
They were all required to be out of the fortress by
sunset anyway.

He watched two peasant-types pass by and fell

in behind them, dredging up his mannerism training and putting it to use.

Like most Cultural Survey Service operatives, he had been put through in-depth training in human behavior and mannerisms, the rationale being that humans will behave like humans, no matter how long they have been separated from the rest of the race. There would always be exceptions, of course, but in general the CS theory had been proven correct on many a cut-off splinter world. Dalt had been taught to utilize an array of subtle non-specific behavioral cues to give him an aura of *belonging* in any milieu. Calling on that training now as he walked the streets of Overlord Mekk's fortress, he appeared to be a civilian who was used to traveling within these walls and who knew exactly where he was going.

Actually, he had no idea where he was going, but knew he did not want to go through the gate and down to the village, which was where the two men he was following were headed. He turned off at an intersection and went hunting for barracks or any other place where the troops might be gathered at this time of day.

It was nearly sunset when he found a group of them clustered about the door to a tavern of sorts, sipping mugs of ale and laughing. They had no doubt just come off the day watch. Dalt approached and stood slightly off to one side, affecting an air of humble deference to their positions as defenders of the Overlord.

Finally, someone deigned to notice him.

"What are you standing there for?" a trooper asked in a surly tone. He was dark, middle-aged, with a big belly and no hint of kindness or mirth in his laughter.

Dalt avoided eye contact and said, "Sir, I—"

"Looking for a drink?"

The trooper casually flipped the dregs of his mug at Dalt who could have easily dodged the flying liquid, but chose instead to let it spatter across his jerkin.

He carefully brushed himself off while the troopers roared and slapped the fat one on the back. Adjusting his clothes, he checked on the position of the blaster tucked inside his belt—it was against all CSS regulations to carry one, but he knew Mekk's troops were selected for their brutality and, regulations or no regulations, he had no intention of letting some barbarian swine like this one stick a dirk between his ribs just for fun.

"I'm searching for Captain Ghentren," he said when the laughter had quieted enough for him to be heard.

"You won't find him here," the fat one said, more kindly disposed now toward a man he had embarrassed and degraded.

"I bring some of his personal effects from Lord Kitru's realm," Dalt said. "He is awaiting them."

"Well, then you'd better rush off and find him, little man!" the fat one roared and went to refill his mug.

Dalt took a gamble. "I'll find him sooner or later, and I'm sure he'll be glad to learn of all the help I received in carrying out his errand."

This brought a sudden change in mood to the group of troopers. Their laughter died and the fat enlisted man turned and studied Dalt. The gamble had paid off—Ghentren was not known as one of the more easy-going officers.

"He's quartered in the red building over there," he said, pointing. "But he's overseeing wall patrol now. Should be back right after sunset."

Dalt turned to see which building he meant, then walked the other way, leaving an uneasy knot of troopers behind him. He was drawing a mental map and picking out easy landmarks for Jon to follow in the darkness when a bell sounded from the direction of the gate—the warning signal for all civilians to leave the fortress.

He quickened his pace.

XV

Jon found waiting for Dalt an agonizing experience. If Dalt was captured by the troopers for being inside the fortress without a pass, he would be dealt with harshly—perhaps lethally—and it would all be entirely the tery's fault.

And it had all been a bluff.

If Tlad had held firm and refused to go up into the fortress, Jon knew he would have had no choice but to place the bomb as he had originally promised. But his intransigent posture, fueled by his genuine craving for revenge, had fooled Tlad.

As he watched the sky darken through the grate, he became increasingly apprehensive. He was about to promise himself that if Tlad returned unharmed he would abandon all plans to kill Ghentren, that he would give up restoring the balance in exchange for Tlad's well-being, when he heard footsteps approaching. A voice above him whispered.

"Open up! Quick!" It was Tlad's voice.

Bursting with relief, Jon strained and pushed the grate upward until Tlad could slip under it, then let it down slowly. Both huddled in the damp drainage pipe in silence for a few heartbeats, then returned to the ventilation shaft and descended to the observation corridor.

"You found him?" Jon asked.

His resolution of a moment before was a quickly fading memory. Knowledge that the debt incurred by the slaughter of the two beings in the world he had loved most was soon to be settled vibrated through his body, blotting out all other considerations.

Dalt nodded in the dim glow that washed through the transparent wall from the Hole.

"Found him. But I'm warning you—don't do it. You won't be the same man when you come back."

"Tell me where he is." The tery's mind was on a single course now.

With obvious reluctance, Dalt knelt and drew a map in the dust on the floor, showing Jon which way to best travel without being seen.

"He's in a red building here," he said, pointing, "Just where in that particular building he'll be, I don't know." He looked up and caught the tery's eyes. "It's too risky for you, Jon. Don't go."

"I won't take long," Jon said.

He quickly turned away from Tlad's troubled face and glided smoothly up the ladder into the growing darkness above. He waited in the storm drain until dusk faded into night, then slipped up into the alley.

Jon was consumed by a terrible urgency as he moved from shadow to shadow along the narrow, ill-lit streets. He had to find Captain Ghentren. Everything would be put right when that man was dead—the sun would move more smoothly across the sky, the breeze would blow cleaner, the world would have brighter days. Ghentren had become a blot on all Creation, a defect that had to be removed.

Then . . . only then would everything again be as it should be. The end of Ghentren consumed him, obsessed him, inflamed him—

He spotted the red building dead ahead. Jon had to detour through three back alleys to avoid crossing a wide courtyard lined with off-duty troopers. Reaching the building, he stole from window to window, listening for a voice, looking for a face when he dared.

He found the captain in a corner room. He was seated on his cot. A woman stood before him.

"Pay me first," she said, giggling as she lifted the hem of her skirt. "That was our agreement."

"I could have you arrested for being within the walls after dark, you little sow," Ghentren said with a playful smile as he reached into the coin pouch at his belt.

"My sisters and I have been an exception to that rule, long before you ever came here."

A table with a lamp and a low wooden stool completed the furnishings of the room. The door to the left was closed and bolted.

Jon was through the window and standing in the middle of the room before either of them noticed him. Ghentren shot to his feet as the girl began to scream but the tery was faster than either of them. With a single motion he shoved the girl back into the corner of the room where she huddled stunned and gasping for breath, then ripped the captain's reaching arm away from the hilt of his sword. Wrapping the fingers of his right hand around the man's throat, he lifted him clear of the floor and held him there.

"Look at me!" Jon said in a low growl, his face a hand's breadth from the captain's.

Ghentren's eyes, already wide with fear, widened further with shock at the sound of coherent speech from the tery's throat.

Jon stared at him. He seemed to be surrounded by a bloody haze that narrowed the world's population to two individuals, the captain and himself, forever locked in combat. Nothing else existed at this moment, nothing else mattered. He could feel within his body the arrows that had killed his father, feel across his throat the bite of the blade that had cut off his mother's life. He had hungered for this moment.

"Do you remember me?" he hissed into the captain's terrified face.

Ghentren's mouth worked but no words passed the lips. He shook his head: No, he absolutely did not remember the beast that held him by the throat.

"Remember the two teries you killed near a cave when you were working for Kitru?" Jon said.

He wanted Ghentren to remember. He must know *why* he was dying. The captain shook his head again.

"Your archers killed the male and your swordsman nearly beheaded the female—remember?"

Still no light of recognition in the eyes.

Jon was aghast. Did it mean so little to this man? He had forever changed Jon's world, made it a dark, lonely and fearful place by killing the two people he had loved most, and Ghentren didn't even *remember* it! What sort of creature *was* this?

"And the son, the young tery who charged you with a club—remember what you did to him? Remember how you chased him and sliced him and left him for dead?"

Jon caught an impression of movement out of the corner of his right eye. The girl, still cringing in the corner, was rising slowly to her feet. He ignored her, and brought Ghentren's face closer to his own until their noses almost touched.

"He did not die!"

Ghentren remembered something now. It showed in his eyes. And there was something else: a kind of irrational disbelief that this could really be happening, that this bestial creature could actually be in his own quarters, speaking to him, *threatening* him! Jon acted to erase all doubt by tightening the pressure on Ghentren's windpipe.

"And what is more, I am not the dumb animal you thought. I am a *man!* And I have come to collect on a debt—*in kind!*"

Horror and mortal fear of a slow, agonizing death accentuated the terror already distorting the captain's features. Jon hoped he was feeling what his mother felt as she saw Ghentren and his men charge into her home with drawn swords.

More movement to Jon's right—the girl was edging along the wall toward the door. He was about to reach for her, to thrust her back into the corner, when the man in his grasp did something that took the tery completely by surprise.

The captain began to cry.

Tears rolled from his eyes as his body jerked with deep, pitiful sobs. Jon let him go and watched as he sank to his knees and begged in a choked voice for mercy. His pants were soaked with urine down both legs and he shook with unconcealed terror.

Feeling as if he had been suddenly doused with icy water, Jon took a step backward and regarded his nemesis. The red haze was gone, as was the rage. He was aware of the woman somewhere in the room behind him, bending toward the floor, but his mind was now completely filled with wonder at his own stupidity.

Was this the man whose death was to restore the balance? Was this blubbering, groveling creature even worth slaying?

What a fool he had been! Risking Tlad's life and bartering with the lives of all the Talents just to come and personally put an end to the days of one man. Tlad had been right—Ghentren wasn't worth it. He was scum. Jon's right hand felt unclean now after touching him . . .

Turning to go, he caught a blur of movement behind him. Before he could react, the back of his head seemed to explode. His knees gave, and as he fell he saw the girl standing there with the heavy wooden stool in her hand. He tried to rise but Ghentren was up and had grabbed the stool from the girl. Jon saw him raise it, saw it descend,

felt a crushing blow to his head, then saw nothing
. . . but he could still hear the captain's voice.

"You think you're a man, do you? We'll have to
find a fitting end for a hairy piece of dung like
you!"

Jon felt another blow, and the voice faded away.

XVI

. . . pain in his hands and in his feet . . . can't move them . . . the cool night air on his face . . . opening his eyes and looking down on a cheering, jostling crowd of troopers . . . and beyond them, others . . . all watching him . . . a loud gong echoing through the darkness . . .

. . . there's wood against his spine and against the backs of his outstretched arms . . . he looks right and left and sees spikes through his palms, fixing him to the wood . . . the same with his feet . . . and there's rope around each of his arms to keep his considerable weight from sagging too much and ripping free of the spikes . . .

. . . he hangs outside the fortress on a cross of wood . . .

. . . a voice below, taunting him . . . Captain Ghentren . . . the man he had spared stands safe now below . . .

"Are you awake, tery? Good! I don't want you to

sleep through this. We're honoring you, in a way.
You think you're a man, so we've raised you like
one. Feel the spikes in your hands and feet? That's
the way a human heretic dies. Pretending to be
human makes you a heretic. But since you're really a tery, we can't just leave you hanging there."

. . . there's kindling below, around the foot of
the cross . . . Captain Ghentren puts a torch to it
and steps back . . .

"See this? Fire. That's the way we rid ourselves
of filthy teries!"

. . . there is no hope of escape, or of anyone
saving him . . . he sees that now . . . and resigns
himself to what must be . . .

. . . light flickers off the faces of the men circled
below . . . Ghentren the parent-slayer grins up at
him . . . his face joyously hate-filled as he cheers
the flames upward along with the others . . .

. . . men . . . humans . . . he had so wanted to
be accepted as one of them . . .

. . . one of *them?* . . . why?

. . . look at them . . . look at their glee in the
face of another's agony . . . why had he wanted to
be a man at all? . . . better to have stayed a tery
forever . . .

. . . and then he remembers Tlad and Komak
and Rab . . . and Adriel, of course . . . it was their
acceptance he had craved . . . they were the humanity he had sought . . .

"I AM A MAN!" he shouts to those below as the
heat builds . . .

Suddenly there is silence . . . awed . . . shaken.

"I AM ONE OF YOU!"

. . . someone laughs, nervously . . . then an-

other . . . a stone flies out of the darkness and
lands on his right shoulder . . . then there is laughter and jeering all around . . . and more stones . . .

. . . he has to close his eyes now . . the heat is
too much . . . the fur on his legs is burning, but
the pain seems far away . . . the Talents . . . he
failed them . . . now Mekk will get the weapons
and exterminate them once and for all . . . . they
counted on him and he failed them . . . what can
they do now?

. . . the pain comes nearer . . . each breath
seems to contain flame . . . thoughts run together . . .

Am I dying as a man or as a beast? . . . does it
matter? . . . does anyone in the laughing darkness
out there know that a man is dying up here? . . .
does anyone care? . . . will anyone remember me?
. . . does anyone who knows me know that I am
dying? . . . will the Talents curse me and hate me
for failing them? . . . not Adriel . . . please don't
let her hate me . . . please let someone remember
me fondly after I'm gone . . .

Please let someone say, just once, that here was
a good man . . .

All became pain and confusion, and soon the
pain passed beyond all comprehension . . .

. . . leaving only confusion.

XVII

Jon was late.

The sound of the gong made Dalt uneasy. There was something ominous in its tone, and Jon was late. He could have been back and forth to Ghentren's quarters three times by now. Faintly-heard laughter drifted in from the far end of the alley as Dalt waited under the grate. A passing voice shouted something about "a special burning."

That did it. He was frightened now. Jon was in trouble—he was sure of it.

He pressed up against the grate but still could not budge it. Leaving the latching lever in the open position, Dalt descended as rapidly as he knew how and hit the floor running. If he was wrong, Jon would be able to lift the grate and get down the airshaft on his own when he returned. If his suspicions were correct and Jon was in trouble . . .

There had to be something he could do.

The ceaseless struggle for existence in the Hole went barely noticed through the viewing wall to his right as he ran down the corridor. He came to the opening where the rocks had been pulled away and climbed out into the fresh night air.

Rab was gone. He was supposed to be waiting here but Dalt could find no trace of him. There was no time to waste looking for him. It was perhaps two kilometers along a ravine and up a hill to the fortress. Dalt ran all the way.

He saw the flames as soon as he topped the bank of the ravine, but wouldn't allow himself to think that Jon might be in any way involved. They leaped high, those flames—six or seven meters into the air. The conflagration stood to the right of the gate, a short distance from the outer wall, and was surrounded by a knot of people.

Why the fire? That was the crucifixtion spot. They burned teries and Talents in the pit on the far side of the fortress. What was going on?

A trooper shouted to him as he ran up.

"Where have you been? All villagers are to report to the gate when they hear the gong. You should know that by now. Get up there and learn a lesson!"

Dalt made no reply as he hurried on. He noted that the civilians were keeping to the rear of the circle of spectators, most with averted eyes. The front ranks were completely taken up by troopers, cheering, laughing, and drinking as they watched the burning body affixed to the cross.

He suspended all emotion as he pushed his way to the front to confirm his worst fears. No facial features were left on that charred corpse. But none were needed. The barrel chest, the shape of the head and legs . . . unmistakable.

Jon, the tery, the man, was dead.

There were voices around him and Dalt heard them as if from a great distance.

"—hear he could have killed the captain but didn't—"

"—and she says he had Ghentren up in the air by the throat and just let him go—"

"—'s like they say, these teries are stupid. Could have killed him clean and got out the same's he came in, however that was, and didn't do it. Deserve to die, all of 'em—"

"—oughtta crucify them more often—"

"—better'n just running them through and then burning them—"

Dalt felt his control begin to slip. He feared he might fly into an uncontrollable rage, might grab his blaster and start burning holes into these savages. But he did not touch his blaster. He left it hidden in his belt as an icy calm slipped over him.

He turned quietly away and strode toward the forest.

He felt dead inside. Everything had gone wrong on this accursed planet and this was the final blow. He had grown to love Jon and now he was dead, horribly dead. If only . . .

If only! There was a long string of *if-only*'s trailing through his mind, starting with the Teratols and their perversity, on through his CSS superior's refusal to authorize a protectorate, up to and including his own attempts to discourage Jon from trying to settle his personal score with Ghentren.

If only he had tried a little harder, maybe he

could have convinced him not to go . . . if only he hadn't tried so hard, maybe Jon wouldn't have hesitated at the crucial moment, maybe he'd have dispatched that captain and been back in a few minutes' time. Or perhaps he would have hesitated anyway because of the innate nobility that made him Jon. Dalt didn't know.

One thing he did know, however, was that Jon would still be alive if a protectorate had been set up. The CSS was at fault there. Always hesitating, always stepping back, always mincing around . . . rotten hands-off policy. Well, he was through with a hands-off policy as of this moment. Those scum back there liked fire, did they? Well, then they'd see some fire, more than they'd ever—

"You're to stay by the gate until you're dismissed!" said a trooper standing back from the crowd.

He started to move forward to block Dalt's path, then retreated. Perhaps there was something in the way Dalt held himself, something in the way he moved; perhaps the trooper caught a glimpse of Dalt's white, tight-lipped face. Whatever it was, the lone sentry decided to let this one pass without an argument.

Not too much further along, Dalt came upon a staring, motionless figure, standing in the darkness, transfixed by the flames.

"Rab!" Dalt shook his shoulder roughly. "Rab, are you all right?"

Rab blinked twice, then staggered. For a heartbeat or two, he didn't seem to know where he was. Then he recognized Dalt.

"Tlad! I saw it all! It was horrible! They're all

monsters in that fortress! What they did to Jon
. . . I never dreamed anyone could—"

Dalt put a hand over his mouth to silence him.
When he spoke, his voice was cold, flat, emotion-
less.

"I know. We've got to tell the rest of the Talents."

"They already know. I acted as a conduit and
transmitted everything I saw back to them. They
saw it all through me. They are all witnesses!"

"Adriel?"

Rab glanced back at the dancing flames outside
Mekk's gate.

"Komak will tell her. Tonight I was glad she was
without the Talent. We've lost a good friend, Tlad—
another life Mekk will answer for some day. But
for now, what do we do?"

"We split up. You go to your people in the
forest and stay there. No one is to venture near
the fortress until morning. *No one!*"

Rab looked at him questioningly, but before he
could speak, Dalt hurried on.

"Remember what I told you awhile back when
you asked me how to fight a myth?"

Rab's brow furrowed momentarily, then he nodded. "Another myth, you said—a bigger and better one."

"Right! And the new one starts here. Tonight. It
will concern a rough-looking creature everyone
persecuted because he was called a tery, but he
was really a man. How he tried to live in peace as
a man. And how one day he was captured and
died horribly at the hands of his persecutors. You
spread the word about that, Rab. And tell the
world what happened to those who killed him."

"But nothing happened to them!"

"Not yet!"

Rab stared uncomprehendingly at the man he knew as Tlad.

"Don't worry, Rab. I'm not mad. Not quite. But something is going to happen tonight, and I don't want it passed off as a natural catastrophe. I want people to remember tonight and know that it happened for a reason."

"What's going to happen?"

Dalt's face was a mask. "Something I'm going to have to live with the rest of my life."

As Dalt turned and trotted toward the trees, Rab called after him.

"I won't be seeing you again, will I?"

Dalt didn't reply.

Dalt brought his ship to a silent hover over Mekk's fortress. Except for a few sputtering torches, all was dark below. Perhaps a few embers glowed around the base of the cross that held the tery's charred remains, but Dalt could not see them from where he was. The villagers had returned to their frightened hovels far down at the base of the hill. All was quiet.

He pointed up the nose of his slender craft and aimed his ion drive tubes at the fortress. He had to do this *now*. If he gave himself enough time to think, if he actually allowed himself to weigh the risks of firing an ion drive within a planet's atmosphere, he would abandon the whole idea.

But Dalt was not thinking now. He was doing.

He realized that during the course of the rest of his life he would analyze and reanalyze the reasons

for what he was about to do. Eventually he knew
he would conclude that it all hinged upon the
uniqueness of Jon the tery. If anyone else in his
group of contacts on the planet had been immo-
lated outside Mekk's fortress, he would have
grieved, cursed, ground his teeth with the rest of
them, and continued the mission.

But Jon's death had temporarily unhinged Dalt.
There had been something very special about that
rough beast who was a man; something clean,
free, and innocent; a certain incorruptible sane-
ness that was singlular and precious in his experience. And now it was gone—lost to Dalt and the
rest of humanity forever.

Gone . . .

But he would see that it was not forgotten. Jon
deserved better than to have his ashes scattered to
the wind. He deserved a more permanent memo-
rial, an enduring tombstone. And he would have
it.

A long blast from the tubes that drove his craft
through peristellar space would prove disastrous
here in an oxygen-laden atmosphere; the Leason
crystal lining would crack and Dalt and his craft
would become a tiny, short-lived sun. But a
short blast . . . a short blast would obviate the
need for a protectorate; a short blast would also
obviate the need for a CS operative below. It
would have the same net effect as the bomb he
had wanted Jon to plant in the cache: Mekk would
be gone, his fortress would be gone, the cache of
Shaper relics would be gone, and all the poor mad
creatures in the Hole would be gone.

But Dalt knew he wouldn't be leaving pure destruction below. He would be creating, too.

Creating a myth.

All with one short blast.

As he reached his fingertip toward the sensor that would activate the drive, Dalt mentally began composing his letter of resignation from the Cultural Survey Service.

" . . . for wandering brooding in
heaven you'll be . . .
". . . all be . . ."
". . . all be blessed . . ."
". . . with the image of the immolation
seared upon their minds . . ."

EPILOGUE

" . . . with the image of the immolation seared upon their minds, the Talents, led by the Apostle Rab, spread the word: That God had chosen to send his messenger in the form of what was then considered lower life form. God did this to show us that teries were men, too, and that we are all brothers."

"Amazing!" Father Pirella said as he followed Mantha toward the place called God's-Touch. "Our 'messenger' did the same—he came as a member of a persecuted race."

"And was he killed like ours?" Mantha asked.

"Very much so."

"And did God show his wrath then?"

"Wrath? No. God showed his love by forgiving them all."

Mantha considered this briefly. "Perhaps God had less patience with Overlord Mekk. Or perhaps he loved our messenger more."

He pushed aside a branch and suddenly all the foliage was gone. They were standing on a gentle rise. Before them lay God's-Touch—a kilometer-wide expanse of green grass. Whatever had once occupied this spot had been melted and fused by a blast of what must have been almost unimaginable heat.

"God left no doubt as to his feelings in this matter. He laid his finger upon Overlord Mekk's fortress and since that day no one has ever persecuted a tery."

PARD

I

The orbital survey had indicated this clearing as the probable site of the crash, but long-range observation had turned up no signs of wreckage. Steven Dalt was doing no better at close range. Something had landed here with tremendous impact not too long ago: There was a deep furrow, a few of the trees were charred, and the grass had not yet been able to fully cover the earth-scar. So far, so good. But where was the wreckage? He had made a careful search of the trees around the clearing and there was nothing of interest there. It was obvious now that there would be no quick, easy solution to the problem, as he had originally hoped, so he started the half-kilometer trek back to his concealed shuttle-craft.

Topping a leafy rise, he heard a shout off to his left and turned to see a small party of mounted colonists, Tependians by their garb. The oddity of the sight struck him. They were well inside the

Duchy of Bendelema, and that shouldn't be:
Bendelema and Tependia had been at war for
generations. Dalt shrugged and started walking
again. He'd been away for years and it was very
possible that something could have happened in
that time to soften relations between the two duch-
ies. Change was the rule on a splinter world.

One of the colonists pointed an unwieldy apparatus at Dalt and something went *thip* past his
head. Dalt went into a crouch and ran to his right.
There had been at least one change since his departure: Someone had reinvented the crossbow.

The hooves of the Tependian mounts thudded
in pursuit as he raced down the slope into a dank,
twilit grotto, and Dalt redoubled his speed as he
realized how simple it would be for his pursuers to
surround and trap him in this sunken area. He had
to gain the high ground on the other side before
he was encircled. Halfway up the far slope, he was
halted by the sound of hooves ahead of him. They
had succeeded in cutting him off.

Dalt turned and made his way carefully down
the slope. If he could just keep out of sight, they
might think he had escaped the ring they had
thrown around the grotto. Then, when it got dark—

A bolt smashed against a stone by his foot. "There
he is!" someone cried, and Dalt was on the run
again. .

He began to weigh the situation in his mind. If
he kept on running, they were bound to keep on
shooting at him, and one of them just might put a
bolt through him. If he stopped running, he might
have a chance. They might let him off with his life.
Then he remembered that he was dressed in serf's

clothing and serfs who ran from anyone in uniform were usually put to the sword. Dalt kept running.

Another bolt flashed by, this one ripping some bark off a nearby tree. They were closing in—they were obviously experienced at this sort of work—and it wouldn't be long before Dalt was trapped at the lowest point of the grotto, with nowhere else to go.

Then he saw the cave mouth, a wide, low arch of darkness just above him on the slope. It was about a meter and a half high at its central point. With a shower of crossbow bolts raining around him, Dalt quickly ducked inside.

It wasn't much of a cave. In the dark and dampness Dalt soon found that it rapidly narrowed to a tunnel too slender for his shoulders to pass. There was nothing else for him to do but stay as far back as possible and hope for the best . . . which wasn't much no matter how he looked at it. If his pursuers didn't feel like coming in to drag him out, they could just sit back and fill the cave with bolts. Sooner or later one would have to strike him. Dalt peered out the opening to see which it would be.

But his five pursuers were doing nothing. They sat astride their mounts and stared dumbly at the cave mouth. One of the party unstrung his crossbow and began to strap it to his back. Dalt had no time to wonder at their behavior, for in that instant he realized he had made a fatal error. He was in a cave on Kwashi, and there was hardly a cave on Kwashi that didn't house a colony of alarets.

He jumped into a crouch and sprinted for the outside. He'd gladly take his chances against crossbows rather than alarets any day. But a warm furry oval fell from the cave ceiling and landed on his head as he began to move. As his ears roared and his vision turned orange and green and yellow, Steve Dalt screamed in agony and fell to the cave floor.

Hearing that scream, the five Tependian scouts shook their heads and turned and rode away.

It was dark when he awoke and he was cold and alone . . . and alive. That last part surprised him when he remembered his situation, and he lost no time in crawling out of the cave and into the clean air under the open stars. Hesitantly, he reached up and peeled from his scalp the shrunken, desiccated remains of one dead alaret. He marveled at the thing in his hand. Nowhere in the history of Kwashi, neither in the records of its long-extinct native race nor in the memory of anyone in its degenerated splinter colony, had there ever been mention of someone surviving the attack of an alaret.

The original splinter colonists had found artifacts of an ancient native race soon after their arrival. The culture had reached preindustrial levels before it was unaccountably wiped out; a natural cataclysm of some sort was given the blame. But among the artifacts were found some samples of symbolic writing, and one of these samples— evidently aimed at the children of the race—strongly warned against entering any cave. It seemed that a creature described as the *killing-thing-on-the-ceilings-of-caves* would attack anything that entered. The writing warned: "Of every thousand struck down, nine hundred and ninety-nine will die."

William Alaret, a settler with some zoological training, had heard the translation and decided to find out just what it was all about. He went into the first cave he could find and emerged seconds later, screaming and clawing at the furry little thing on his head. He became the first of many fatalities attributed to the *killing-thing-on-the-ceilings-of-caves*, which were named "alarets" in his honor.

Dalt threw the alaret husk aside, got his bearings, and headed for his hidden shuttlecraft. He anticipated little trouble this time. No scouting party, if any were abroad at this hour, would be likely to spot him, and Kwashi had few large carnivores.

The ship was as he had left it. He lifted slowly to fifty thousand meters and then cut in the orbital thrust. That was when he first heard the voice.

("Hello, Steve.")

If it hadn't been for the G-forces against him at that moment, Dalt would have leaped out of his chair in surprise.

("This pressure is quite uncomfortable, isn't it?") the voice said, and Dalt realized that it was coming from inside his head. The thrust automatically cut off as orbit was reached and his stomach gave its familiar free-fall lurch.

("Ah! this is much better.")

"What's going on?" Dalt cried aloud as he glanced frantically about. "Is this someone's idea of a joke?"

("No joke, Steve. I'm what's left of the alaret that landed on your head back in that cave. You're quite lucky, you know. Mutual death is a sure result—most of the time, at least—whenever a creature of high-level intelligence is a target for pairing.")

I'm going mad! Dalt thought.

("No, you're not, at least not yet. But it is a possibility if you don't sit back and relax and accept what's happened to you.")

Dalt leaned back and rested his eyes on the growing metal cone that was the Star Ways Corporation mothership, on the forward viewer. The glowing signal on the console indicated that the bigger ship had him in traction and was reeling him in.

"Okay, then. Just what *has* happened to me?" He felt a little ridiculous speaking out loud in an empty cabin.

("Well, to put it in a nutshell: You've got yourself a roommate, Steve. From now on, you and I will be sharing your body.")

"In other words, I've been invaded!"

("That's a loaded term, Steve, and not quite accurate. I'm not really taking anything from you except some of your privacy, and that shouldn't really matter since the two of us will be so intimately associated.")

"And just what gives you the right to invade my mind?" Dalt asked quickly, then added: "—*and* my privacy?"

("Nothing gives me the right to do so, but there are extenuating circumstances. You see, a few hours ago I was a furry, lichen-eating cave slug with no intelligence to speak of—")

"For a slug you have a pretty good command of the language!" Dalt interrupted.

("No better and no worse than yours, for I derive whatever intelligence I have from you. You see, we alarets, as you call us, invade the nervous system of any creature of sufficient size that comes near enough. It's an instinct with us. If the creature is a dog, then we wind up with the intelligence of a dog—that *particular* dog. If it's a human and if he survives, as you have done, the invading alaret finds himself possessing a very high degree of intelligence.")

"You used the word 'invade' yourself just then."

("Just an innocent slip, I assure you. I have no intention of taking over. That would be quite immoral.")

Dalt laughed grimly. "What would an ex-slug know about morality?"

("With the aid of your faculties I can reason now, can I not? And if I can reason, why can't I arrive at a moral code? This is your body and I am here only because of blind instinct. I have the ability to take control—not without a struggle, of course—but it would be immoral to attempt to do so. I couldn't vacate your mind if I wanted to, so you're stuck with me, Steve. Might as well make the best of it.")

"We'll see how 'stuck' I am when I get back to the ship," Dalt muttered. "But I'd like to know how you got into my brain."

("I'm not exactly sure of that myself. I know the path I followed to penetrate your skull—if you had the anatomical vocabulary I could describe it to you, but my vocabulary is your vocabulary and yours is very limited in that area.")

"What do you expect? I was educated in cultural studies, not medicine!"

("It's not important anyway. I remember almost nothing of my existence before entering your skull, for it wasn't until then that I first became truly aware.")

Dalt glanced at the console and straightened up in his seat. "Well, whatever you do, go away for now. I'm ready to dock and I don't want to be distracted."

("Gladly. You have a most fascinating organism and I have much exploring to do before I become fully acquainted with it. So long for now, Steve. It's nice knowing you.")

A thought drifted through Dalt's head: *If I'm going nuts, at least I'm not doing it halfheartedly!*

II

Barre was there to meet him at the dock. "No luck, Steve?"

Dalt shook his head and was about to add a comment when he noticed Barre staring at him with a strange expression.

"What's the matter?"

"You won't believe me if I tell you," Barre replied. He took Dalt's arm and led him into a nearby men's room and stood him in front of a mirror.

Dalt saw what he expected to see: a tall, muscular man in the garb of a Kwashi serf. Tanned face, short, glossy brown hair . . . Dalt suddenly flexed his neck to get a better look at the top of his head. Tufts of hair were missing in a roughly oval patch on his scalp. He ran his hand over it and a light rain of brown hair showered past his eyes. With successive strokes, the oval patch became completely denuded and a shiny expanse of scalp reflected the ceiling lights into the mirror.

"Well, I'll be damned! A bald spot!"

("Don't worry, Steve,") said the voice in his head, ("the roots aren't dead. The hair will grow back.")

"It damn well better!" Dalt said aloud.

"It damn well better what?" Barre asked puzzledly.

"Nothing," Dalt replied. "Something dropped onto my head in a cave down there and it looks like it's given me a bald spot." He realized then that he would have to be very careful about talking to his invader; otherwise, even if he really wasn't crazy, he'd soon have everyone on the ship believing he was.

"Maybe you'd better see the doc," Barre suggested.

"I intend to, believe me. But first I've got to report to Clarkson. I'm sure he's waiting."

"You can bet on it." Barre had been a research head on the brain project and was well acquainted with Dirval Clarkson's notorious impatience.

The pair walked briskly toward Clarkson's office. The rotation of the huge conical ship gave the effect of one-G.

"Hi, Jean," Dalt said with a smile as he and Barre entered the anteroom of Clarkson's office. Jean was Clarkson's secretary-receptionist and she and Dalt had entertained each other on the trip out . . . the more interesting games had been played during the sleep-time hours.

She returned his smile. "Glad you're back in one piece." Dalt realized that from her seated position she couldn't see the bald spot. Just as well for the moment. He'd explain it to her later.

Jean spoke into the intercom: "Mr. Dalt is here."

"Well, send him in!" squawked a voice. "Send him in!"

Dalt grinned and pushed through the door to Clarkson's office, with Barre trailing behind. A huge, graying man leaped from behind a desk and stalked forward at a precarious angle.

"Dalt! Where the hell have you been? You were supposed to go down, take a look, and then come back up. You could have done the procedure three times in the period you took. And what happened to your head?" Clarkson's speech was in its usual rapidfire form.

"Well, this—"

"Never mind that now! What's the story? I can tell right now that you didn't find anything, because Barre is with you. If you'd found the brain he'd be off in some corner now nursing it like a misplaced infant! Well, tell me! How does it look?"

Dalt hesitated, not quite sure whether the barrage had come to an end. "It doesn't look good," he said finally.

"And why not?"

"Because I couldn't find a trace of the ship itself. Oh, there's evidence of some sort of craft having been there a while back, but it must have gotten off-planet again, because there's not a trace of wreckage to be found."

Clarkson looked puzzled. "Not even a trace?"

"Nothing."

The project director pondered this a moment, then shrugged. "We'll have to figure that one out later. But right now you should know that we picked up another signal from the brain's life-support system while you were off on your joy-ride—"

"It wasn't a joyride," Dalt declared. A few moments with Clarkson always managed to rub his nerves raw. "I ran into a pack of unfriendly locals and had to hide in a cave."

"Be that as it may," Clarkson said, returning to his desk chair, "we're now certain that the brain, or what's left of it, is on Kwashi."

"Yes, but where on Kwashi? It's not exactly an asteroid, you know."

"We've almost pinpointed its location," Barre broke in excitedly. "Very close to the side you inspected."

"It's in Bendelema, I hope," Dalt said.

"Why?" Clarkson asked.

"Because when I was on cultural survey down there I posed as a soldier of fortune—a mercenary of sorts—and Duke Kile of Bendelema was a former employer. I'm known and liked in Bendelema. I'm not at all popular in Tependia because they're the ones I fought against. I repeat: It's in Bendelema, I hope."

Clarkson nodded. "It's in Bendelema."

"Good!" Dalt exhaled with relief. "That makes everything much simpler. I've got an identity in Bendelema: Racso the mercenary. At least that's a starting place."

"And you'll start tomorrow," Clarkson said. "We've wasted too much time as it is. If we don't get that prototype back and start coming up with some pretty good reasons for the malfunction, Star

Ways just might cancel the project. There's a lot riding on you, Dalt. Remember that."

Dalt turned toward the door. "Who'll let me forget?" he remarked with a grim smile. "I'll check in with you before I leave."

"Good enough," Clarkson said with a curt nod, then turned to Barre. "Hold on a minute, Barre. I want to go over a few things with you." Dalt gladly closed the door on the pair.

"It's almost lunchtime," said a feminine voice behind him. "How about it?"

In a single motion, Dalt spun, leaned over Jean's desk, and gave her a peck on the lips. "Sorry, can't. It may be noon to all of you on ship-time, but it's some hellish hour of the morning to me. I've got to drop in on the doc, then I've got to get some sleep."

But Jean wasn't listening. Instead, she was staring fixedly at the bald spot on Dalt's head. "Steve!" she cried. "What happened?"

Dalt straightened up abruptly. "Nothing much. Something landed on it while I was below and the hair fell out. It'll grow back, don't worry."

"I'm not worried about that," she said, standing up and trying to get another look. But Dalt kept his head high. "Did it hurt?"

"Not at all. Look, I hate to run off like this, but I've got to get some sleep. I'm going back down tomorrow."

Her face fell. "So soon?"

"I'm afraid so. Why don't we make it for dinner tonight. I'll drop by your room and we'll go from there. The caf isn't exactly a restaurant, but if we get there late we can probably have a table all to ourselves."

"And after that?" she asked coyly.

"I'll be damned if we're going to spend my last night on ship for who-knows-how-long in the vid theater!"

Jean smiled. "I was hoping you'd say that."

("What odd physiological rumblings that female stirs in you!") the voice said as Dalt walked down the corridor to the medical offices. He momentarily broke stride at the sound of it. He'd almost forgotten that he had company.

"That's none of your business!" he muttered through tight lips.

("I'm afraid much of what you do is my business. I'm not directly connected with you emotionally, but physically . . . what you feel, I feel; what you see, I see; what you taste—")

"Okay! Okay!"

("You're holding up rather well, actually. Better than I would have expected.")

"Probably my cultural-survey training. They taught me how to keep my reactions under control when faced with an unusual situation."

("Glad to hear it. We may well have a long relationship ahead of us if you don't go the way of most high-order intelligences and suicidally reject me. We can look on your body as a small business and the two of us as partners.")

"Partners!" Dalt said, somewhat louder than he wished. Luckily, the halls were deserted. "This is *my* body!"

("If it will make you happier, I'll revise my

analogy: You're the founder of the company and I've just bought my way in. How's that sound, Partner?")

"Lousy!"

("Get used to it,") the voice singsonged.

"Why bother? You won't be in there much longer. The doc'll see to that!"

("He won't find a thing, Steve.")

"We'll see."

The door to the medical complex swished open when Dalt touched the operating plate and he passed into a tiny waiting room.

"What can we do for you, Mr. Dalt?" the nurse-receptionist said. Dalt was a well-known figure about the ship by now.

He inclined his head toward the woman and pointed to the bald spot. "I want to see the doc about this. I'm going below tomorrow and I want to get this cleared up before I do. So if the doc's got a moment, I'd like to see him."

The nurse smiled. "Right away." At the moment, Dalt was a very important man. He was the only one on ship legally allowed on Kwashi. If he thought he needed a doctor, he'd have one.

A man in a traditional white medical coat poked his head through one of the three doors leading from the waiting room, in answer to the nurse's buzz.

"What is it, Lorraine?" he asked.

"Mr. Dalt would like to see you, Doctor."

He glanced at Dalt. "Of course. Come in, Mr. Dalt. I'm Dr. Graves." The doctor showed him into a small, book-and-microfilm-lined office. "Have a seat, will you? I'll be with you in a minute."

Graves exited by another door and Dalt was alone . . . almost.

("He has quite an extensive library here, doesn't he?") said the voice. Dalt glanced at the shelves and noticed printed texts that must have been holdovers from the doctor's student days and microfilm spools of the latest clinical developments. ("You would do me a great service by asking the doctor if you could borrow some of his more basic texts.")

"What for? I thought you knew all about me."

("I know quite a bit now, it's true, but I'm still learning and I'll need a vocabulary to explain things to you now and then.")

"Forget it. You're not going to be around that long."

Dr. Graves entered then. "Now. What seems to be the problem, Mr. Dalt?"

Dalt explained the incident in the cave. "Legend has it—and colonial experience seems to confirm it—that 'of every thousand struck down, nine hundred and ninety-nine will die.' I was floored by an alaret but I'm still kicking and I'd like to know why."

("I believe I've already explained that by luck of a random constitutional factor, your nervous system didn't reject me.")

Shut up! Dalt mentally snarled.

The doctor shrugged. "I don't see the problem. You're alive and all you've got to show for your encounter is a bald spot, and even that will disappear—it's bristly already. I can't tell you why you're alive because I don't know how these alarets kill their victims. As far as I know, no one's done any research on them. So why don't you just forget about it and stay out of caves."

"It's not that simple, Doc." Dalt spoke carefully. He'd have to phrase things just right; if he came right out and told the truth, he'd sound like a flaming schiz. "I have this feeling that something seeped into my scalp, maybe even into my head. I feel this thickness there." Dalt noticed the slightest narrowing of the doctor's gaze. "I'm not crazy," he said hurriedly. "You've got to admit that the alaret did something there—the bald spot proves it. Couldn't you make a few tests or something? Just to ease my mind."

The doctor nodded. He was satisfied that Dalt's fears had sufficient basis in reality, and the section-eight gleam left his eyes. He led Dalt into the adjoining room and placed a cubical helmetlike apparatus over his head. A click, a buzz, and the helmet was removed. Dr. Graves pulled out two small transparencies and shoved them into a viewer. The screen came to life with two views of the inside of Dalt's skull: a lateral and an anterior-posterior.

"Nothing to worry about," he said after a moment of study. "I scanned you for your own peace of mind. Take a look."

Dalt looked, even though he didn't know what he was looking for.

("I told you so,") said the voice. ("I'm thoroughly integrated with your nervous system.")

"Well, thanks for your trouble, Doc. I guess I've really got nothing to worry about," Dalt lied.

"Nothing at all. Just consider yourself lucky to be alive if those alarets are as deadly as you say."

("Ask him for the books!") the voice said.

I'm going to sleep as soon as I leave here. You won't get a chance to read them.

("You let me worry about that. Just get the books for me.")

Why should I do you any favors?

("Because I'll see to it that you have one difficult time of getting to sleep. I'll keep you repeating 'get the books, get the books, get the books' until you finally do it.")

I believe you would!

("You can count on it.")

"Doc," Dalt said, "would you mind lending me a few of your books?"

"Like what?"

"Oh, anatomy and physiology, to start."

Dr. Graves walked into the other room and took two large, frayed volumes from the shelves. "What do you want 'em for?"

"Nothing much," Dalt said, taking the books and tucking them under his arm. "Just want to look up a few things."

"Well, just don't forget where you got them. And don't let that incident with the alaret become an obsession with you," the doc said meaningfully.

Dalt smiled. "I've already banished it from my mind."

("That's a laugh!")

Dalt wasted no time in reaching his quarters after leaving the medical offices. He was on the bed before the door could slide back into the closed position. Putting the medical books on the night table, he buried his face in the pillow and immediately dropped off to sleep.

He awoke five hours later, feeling completely refreshed except for his eyes. They felt hot, burning.

("You may return those books anytime you wish,") the voice said.

"Lost interest already?" Dalt yawned, stretching as he lay on the bed.

("In a way, yes. I read them while you were asleep.")

"How the hell did you do that?"

("Quite simple, really. While your mind was sleeping, I used your eyes and hands to read. I digested the information and stored it away in your brain. By the way, there's an awful lot of wasted space in the human brain. You're not living up to anywhere near your potential, Steve. Neither is any other member of your race, I gather.")

"What right have you got to pull something like that with my body?" Dalt said angrily. He sat up and rubbed his eyes.

("*Our* body, you mean.")

Dalt ignored that. "No wonder my eyes are burning! I've been reading when I could have been—*should* have been— sleeping!"

("Don't get excited. You got your sleep and I built up my vocabulary. You're fully rested, so what's your complaint? By the way, I can now tell you how I entered your head. I seeped into your pores and then into your scalp capillaries, which I followed into your parietal emissary veins. These flow through the parietal foramina in your skull and empty into the superior sagittal sinus. From there it was easy to infiltrate your central nervous system.")

Dalt opened his mouth to say that he really didn't care, when he realized that he understood exactly what the voice was saying. He had a clear picture of the described path floating through his mind.

"How come I know what you're talking about? I seem to understand but I don't remember ever hearing those terms before . . . and then again, I do. It's weird."

("It must seem rather odd,") the voice concurred. ("What has happened is that I've made my new knowledge available to you. The result is you experience the fruits of the learning process without having gone through it. You know facts without remembering having learned them.")

"Well," Dalt said, rising to his feet, "at least you're not a complete parasite."

("I resent that! We're partners . . . a symbiosis!")

"I suppose you may come in handy now and then." Dalt sighed.

("I already have.")

"What's that supposed to mean?"

("I found a small neoplasm in your lung—middle lobe on the right. It might well have become malignant.")

"Then let's get back to the doc before it metastatizes!" Dalt said, and idly realized that a few hours ago he would have been worrying about "spread" rather than "metastasis."

("There's no need to worry, Steve. I killed it off.")

"How'd you do that?"

("I just worked through your vascular system and selectively cut off the blood supply to that particular group of cells.")

"Well, thanks, Partner."

("No thanks necessary, I assure you. I did it for my own good as well as yours—I don't relish the idea of walking around in a cancer-ridden body any more than you do!")

Dalt removed his serf clothing in silence. The enormity of what had happened in that cave on Kwashi struck him now with full force. He had a built-in medical watchdog who would keep everything running smoothly. He smiled grimly as he donned ship clothes and suspended from his neck the glowing prismatic gem that he had first worn as Racso and had continued to wear after his cultural-survey assignment on Kwashi had been terminated. He'd have his health but he'd lost his privacy forever. He wondered if it was worth it.

("One other thing, Steve,") said the voice. ("I've accelerated the growth of your hair in the bald spot to maximum.")

Dalt put up a hand and felt a thick fuzz where before there had been only bare scalp. "Hey! You're right! It's really coming in!" He went to the mirror to take a look. "Oh, no!"

("Sorry about that, Steve. I couldn't see it so I wasn't aware there had been a color change. I'm afraid there's nothing I can do about that.")

Dalt stared in dismay at the patch of silvery gray

in the center of his otherwise inky hair. "I look like a freak!"

("You can always dye it.")

Dalt made a disgusted noise.

("I have a few questions, Steve,") the voice said in a hasty attempt to change the subject.

"What about?"

("About why you're going down to that planet tomorrow.")

"I'm going because I was once a member of the Federation cultural-survey team on Kwashi and because the Star Ways Corporation lost an experimental pilot brain down there. They got permission from the Federation to retrieve the brain only on the condition that a cultural-survey man does the actual retrieving."

("That's not what I meant. I want to know what's so important about the brain, just how much of the brain it actually is, and so on.")

"There's an easy way to find out," Dalt said, heading for the door. "We'll just go to the ship's library."

The library was near the hub of the ship and completely computer-operated. Dalt closed himself away in one of the tiny viewer booths and pushed his ID card into the awaited slot.

The flat, dull tones of the computer's voice came from a hidden speaker.

"What do you wish, Mr. Dalt?"

"I might as well go to the route: Let me see everything on the brain project."

Four microspools slid down a tiny chute and landed in the receptacle in front of Dalt. "I'm sorry, Mr. Dalt," said the computer, "but this is all your present status allows you to see."

("That should be enough, Steve. Feed them into the viewer.")

The story that unraveled from the spools was one of biologic and economic daring. Star Ways was fast achieving what amounted to a monopoly of the interstellar-warp-unit market and from there was expanding to peri-stellar drive. But unlike the typical established corporation, SW was pouring money into basic research. One of the prime areas of research was the development of a use for cultured human neural tissue. And James Barre had found a use that held great economic potential.

The prime expense of interstellar commercial travel, whether freight or passenger, was the crew. Good spacers were a select lot and hard to come by; running a ship took a lot of them. There had been many attempts to replace crews with computers but these had invariably failed due either to mass/volume problems or overwhelming maintenance costs. Barre's development of an "artificial" brain—by that he meant structured in vitro—seemed to hold an answer, at least for cargo ships.

After much trial and error with life-support systems and control linkages, a working prototype had finally been developed. A few short hops had been tried with a full crew standing by, and the results had been more than anyone had hoped for. So the prototype was prepared for a long interstellar journey with five scheduled stops—with cargo holds empty, of course. The run had gone quite well until the ship got into the Kwashi area. A single technician had been sent along to insure that nothing went too far awry, and, according to his story, he was sitting in his quarters when the ship suddenly came out of warp with the emergency/abandon ship signals blaring. He wasted no time in getting to a lifeboat and ejecting. The ship made a beeline for Kwashi and disappeared, presumably in a crash. That had been eight months ago.

No more information was available without special clearance.

"Well, that was a waste of time," Dalt said.

"Are you addressing me, Mr. Dalt?" the computer asked.

"No."

("There certainly wasn't much new information there,") the voice agreed.

Dalt pulled his card from the slot, thereby cutting the computer off from this particular viewer booth, before answering. Otherwise it would keep butting in.

"The theories now stand at either malfunction or foul play."

("Why foul play?")

"The spacers' guild, for one," Dalt said, standing. "Competing companies, for another. But since it crashed on a restricted splinter world, I favor the malfunction theory." As he stepped from the booth he glanced at the chronometer on the wall: 1900 hours ship-time. Jean would be waiting.

The cafeteria was nearly deserted when he arrived with Jean and the pair found an isolated table in a far corner.

"I really don't think you should dye your hair at all," Jean was saying as they placed their trays on the table and sat down. "I think that gray patch looks cute in a distinguished sort of way . . . or do I mean distinguished in a cute sort of way?"

Dalt took the ribbing in good-natured silence.

"Steve!" she said suddenly. "How come you're eating with your left hand? I've never seen you do that before."

Dalt looked down. His fork was firmly grasped in his left hand. "That's strange," he said. "I didn't even realize it."

("I integrated a few circuits, so to speak, while you were asleep,") the voice said. ("It seemed rather ridiculous to favor one limb over another. You're now ambidextrous.")

Thanks for telling me, Partner!

("Sorry. I forgot.")

Dalt switched the fork to his right hand and Jean switched the topic of conversation.

"You know, Steve," she said, "you've never told me why you quit the cultural-survey group."

Dalt paused before answering. After the fall of Metep VII, last in a long line of self-styled "Emperors of the Outworlds," a new independent spirit gave rise to a loose organization of worlds called simply the Federation.

"As you know," he said finally, "the Federation has a long-range plan of bringing splinter worlds— willing ones, that is—back into the fold. But it was found that an appalling number had regressed into barbarism. So the cultural surveys were started to evaluate splinter worlds and decide which could be trusted with modern technology. There was another rule which I didn't fully appreciate back then but have come to believe in since, and that's where the trouble began."

"What rule was that?"

"It's not put down anywhere in so many words, but it runs to the effect that if a splinter-world culture had started developing on a path at variance with the rest of humanity, it is to be left alone."

"Sounds like they were making cultural test tubes out of some planets," Jean said.

"Exactly what I thought, but it never bothered me until I surveyed a planet that must, for now, remain nameless. The inhabitants had been developing a psi culture through selective breeding and were actually developing a tangential society. But they were being threatened by the non-psi majority. I pleaded for protective intervention and early admission to the Federation."

"And were turned down, I bet," Jean said.

Dalt nodded. "Right. And I might have gone along if I hadn't become emotionally involved with the psis. That was the first rule I broke. Then I found myself in the middle of a crisis situation that pushed me over the edge. I took decisive action on my own, and then resigned."

"Before you were fired."

"Right again. I broke half a book's worth of rules on that planet. But I can see the Fed's reasoning now. They knew the psi culture wasn't mature enough to withstand exposure to interstellar civilization. They were afraid it would be swallowed up

and lose its unique qualities. They wanted to give
it another few centuries in isolation before opening it up. And they were right in theory. But they
weren't on that planet. I was. And I knew if things
kept on the way they were going, the psi-folk
would be wiped out in less than a generation. So I
. . . did something to make sure that didn't
happen."

"No hard feelings then?"

"Not on my part. I've come to see that there's a
very definite philosophy behind everything the
Federation does. It not only wants to preserve
human diversity, it wants to see it stretched to the
limit. Man was an almost completely homogenized
species before he began colonizing the stars; interstellar travel arrived just in time. Old Earth is still
a good example of what I mean; long ago the
Eastern and Western Alliances fused—something
no one ever thought would happen—and Earth is
just one big faceless, self-perpetuating bureaucracy.
The populace is equally faceless.

"But the man who left for the stars—he's another creature altogether! Once he got away from
the press of other people, once he stopped seeing
what everybody else saw, hearing what everybody
else heard, he began to become an individual again
and to strike out in directions of his own choosing.
The splinter groups carried this out to an extreme
and many failed. But a few survived and the Federation wants to let the successful ones go as far as
they can, both for their own sake and for the sake
of all mankind. Who knows? *Homo superior* may
one day be born on a splinter world."

They took their time strolling back to Dalt's quarters. Once inside, Dalt glanced in the mirror and ran his hand through the gray patch in his hair. "It's still there," he muttered in mock disappointment.

He turned back to Jean and she was already more than half undressed. "You weren't gone all that long, Steve," she said in a low voice, "but I missed you—really missed you."

It was mutual.

III

She was gone when he awakened the next morning but a little note on the night table wished him good luck.

("You should have prepared me for such a sensory jolt,") said the voice. ("I was taken quite by surprise last night.")

"Oh, it's you again," Dalt groaned. "I pushed you completely out of my mind last night, otherwise I'd have been impotent, no doubt."

("I hooked into your sensory input—very stimulating.")

Dalt experienced helpless annoyance. He would have to get used to his partner's presence at the most intimate moments, but how many people could make love knowing that there's a peeping tom at the window with a completely unobstructed view?

("What are we going to do now?")

"Pard," Dalt drawled, "we're gonna git ready to

go below." He went to the closet and pulled from it a worn leather jerkin and a breastplate marked with an empty red circle, the mark of the mercenary. Stiff leather breeches followed and broadsword and metal helm completed the picture. He then dyed his hair for Racso's sake.

"One more thing," he said, and reached up to the far end of the closet shelf. His hand returned clutching an ornate dagger. "This is something new in Racso's armament."

("A dagger?")

"Not just a dagger. It's—"

("Oh, yes. It's also a blaster.")

"How did you know?"

("We're partners, Steve. What you know, I know. I even know why you had it made.")

"I'm listening."

("Because you're afraid you're not as fast as you used to be. You think your muscles may not have quite the tone they used to have when you first posed as Racso. And you're not willing to die looking for an artificial brain.")

"You seem to think you know me pretty well."

("I do. Skin to skin, birth to now. You're the only son of a fairly well-to-do couple on Friendly, had an average childhood and an undistinguished academic career—but you passed the empathy test with high marks and were accepted into the Federation cultural-survey service. You don't speak to your parents anymore. They've never forgiven their baby for running off to go hopping from splinter world to splinter world. You cut yourself off from your home-world but made friends in CS; now you're cut off from CS. You're not a loner by nature but you've adapted. In fact, you have a tremendous capacity to adapt as long as your own personal code of ethics and honor isn't violated—you're very strict about that.")

Dalt sighed. "No secrets anymore, I guess."

("Not from me, at least.")

Dalt planned the time of his arrival in Bendelema Duchy for predawn. He concealed the shuttle and was on the road as the sky began to lighten. Walking with a light saddle slung over his shoulder, he marveled at the full ripe fields of grains and greens on either side of him. Agriculture had always been a hit-or-miss affair on Kwashi and famines were not uncommon, but it looked as if there would be no famine in Bendelema this year. Even the serfs looked well fed.

"What do you think, pard?" Dalt asked.

("Well, Kwashi hasn't got much of a tilt on its axis. They seem to be on their way to the second bumper crop of the year.")

"With the available farming methods, that's unheard of . . . I almost starved here once myself."

("I know that, but I have no explanation for these plump serfs.")

The road made a turn around a small wooded area and the Bendelema keep came into view.

"I see their architecture hasn't improved since I left. The keep still looks like a pile of rocks."

("I wonder why so many retrograde splinter worlds turn to feudalism?") Pard said as they approached the stone structure.

"There are only theories. Could be that feudalism is, in essence, the law of the jungle. When these colonists first land, education of the children has to take a back seat to putting food on the table. That's their first mistake and a tragic one, because once they let technology slide, they're on a down-hill spiral. Usually by the third generation you have a pretty low technological level; the stops are out, the equalizers are gone, and the toughs take over.

"The philosophy of feudalism is one of muscle: Mine is what I can take and hold. It's ordered barbarism. That's why feudal worlds such as Kwashi have to be kept out of the Federation—can you imagine a bunch of those yahoos in command of an interstellar dread-naught? No one's got the time or the money to reeducate them, so they just have to be left alone to work out their own little industrial revolution and so forth. When they're ready, the Fed will give them the option of joining up."

"Ho, mercenary!" someone hailed from the keep gate. "What do you seek in Bendelema?"

"Have I changed that much, Farri?" Dalt answered.

The guard peered at him intensely from the wall, then his face brightened. "Racso! Enter and be welcome! The Duke has need of men of your mettle."

Farri, a swarthy trooper who had gained a few pounds and a few scars since their last meeting, greeted him as he passed through the open gate. "Where's your mount, Racso?" He grinned. "You were never one to walk when you could ride."

"Broke its leg in a ditch more miles back than I care to remember. Had to kill it . . . good steed, too."

"That's a shame. But the Duke'll see that you get a new one."

Dalt's audience with the Duke was disturbingly brief. The lord of the keep had not been as enthusiastic as expected. Dalt couldn't decide whether to put the man's reticence down to distraction with other matters or to suspicion. His son Anthon was a different matter, however. He was truly glad to see Racso.

"Come," he said after mutual greetings were over. "We'll put you in the room next to mine upstairs."

"For a mercenary?"

"For my teacher!" Anthon had filled out since Dalt had seen him last. He had spent many hours with the lad, passing on the tricks of the blade he had learned in his own training days. "I've used your training well, Racso!"

"I hope you didn't stop learning when I left," Dalt said.

"Come down to the sparring field and you'll see that I've not been lax in your absence. I'm a match for you now."

He was more than a match. What he lacked in skill and subtlety he made up with sheer ferocity. Dalt was several times hard-pressed to defend himself, but in the general stroke-and-parry, give-and-take exercises of the practice session he studied Anthon. The lad was still the same as he had remembered him, on the surface: bold, confident, the Duke's only legitimate son and heir to Bendelema, yet there was a new undercurrent. Anthon had always been brutish and a trifle cruel, perfect qualities for a future feudal lord, but there was now an added note of desperation. Dalt hadn't noticed it before and could think of no reason for its presence now. Anthon's position was secure—what was driving him?

After the workout, Dalt immersed himself in a huge tub of hot water, a habit that had earned him the reputation of being a little bit odd the last time around, and then retired to his quarters, where he promptly fell asleep. The morning's long walk carrying the saddle, followed by the vigorous swordplay with Anthon, had drained him.

He awoke feeling stiff and sore.

("I hope those aching muscles cause you sufficient misery.")

"Why do you say that, Pard?" Dalt asked as he kneaded the muscles in his sword arm.

("Because you weren't ready for a workout like that. The clumsy practicing you did on the ship didn't prepare you for someone like Anthon. It's all right if you want to make yourself sore, but don't forget I feel it, too!")

"Well, just cut off pain sensations. You can do it, can't you?"

("Yes, but that's almost as unpleasant as the aching itself.")

"You'll just have to suffer along with me then. And by the way, you've been awful quiet today. What's up?"

("I've been observing, comparing your past impressions of Bendelema keep with what we see now. Either you're a rotten observer or something's going on here . . . something suspicious or something secret or I don't know what.")

"What do you mean by 'rotten observer'?"

("I mean that either your past observations were inaccurate or Bendelema has changed.")

"In what way?"

("I'm not quite sure as yet, but I should know before long. I'm a far more astute observer than you—")

Dalt threw his hands up with a groan. "Not only do I have a live-in busy-body, but an arrogant one to boot!"

There was a knock on the door.

"Come in," Dalt said.

The door opened and Anthon entered. He glanced about the room. "You're alone? I thought I heard you talking—"

"A bad habit of mine of late," Dalt explained hastily. "I think out loud."

Anthon shrugged. "The evening meal will soon be served and I've ordered a place set for you at my father's table. Come."

As he followed the younger man down a narrow flight of roughhewn steps, Dalt caught the heavy, unmistakable scent of Kwashi wine.

A tall, cadaverous man inclined his head as they passed into the dining hall. "Hello, Strench," Dalt said with a smile. "Still the majordomo, I see."

"As long as His Lordship allows," Strench replied.

The Duke himself entered not far behind them and all present remained standing until His Lordship was seated. Dalt found himself near the head of the table and guessed by the ruffled appearance of a few of the court advisers that they had been pushed a little farther from the seat of power than they liked.

"I must thank His Lordship for the honor of allowing a mercenary to sup at his table," Dalt said after a court official had made the customary toast to Bendelema and the Duke's longevity.

"Nonsense, Racso," the Duke replied. "You served me well against Tependia and you've always taken a wholesome interest in my son. You know you will always find welcome in Bendelema."

Dalt inclined his head.

("Why are you bowing and scraping to this slob?")

Shut up, Pard! It's all part of the act.

("But don't you realize how many serfs this barbarian oppresses?")

Shut up, self-righteous parasite!

("Symbiote!")

Dalt rose to his feet and lifted his wine cup. "On the subject of your son, I would like to make a toast to the future Duke of Bendelema: Anthon."

With a sudden animal-like cry, Anthon shot to his feet and hurled his cup to the stone floor. Without a word of explanation, he stormed from the room.

The other diners were as puzzled as Dalt. "Perhaps I said the wrong thing. . . ."

"I don't know what it could have been," the Duke said, his eyes on the red splotch of spilled wine that seeped across the stones. "But Anthon has been acting rather strange of late."

Dalt sat down and raised his cup to his lips.

("I wouldn't quaff too deeply of that beverage, my sharp-tongued partner.")

And why not? Dalt thought, casually resting his lips on the brim.

("Because I think there's something in your wine

that's not in any of the others' and I think we should be careful.")

What makes you suspicious?

("I told you your powers of observation needed sharpening.")

Never mind that! Explain!

("All right. I noticed that your cup was already filled when it was put before you; everyone else's was poured from that brass pitcher.")

The doesn't sound good, Dalt agreed. He started to put the cup down.

("Don't do that! Just wet your lips with a tiny amount and I think I might be able to analyze it by its effect. A small amount shouldn't cause any real harm.")

Dalt did so and waited.

("Well, at least they don't mean you any serious harm,") Pard said finally. ("Not yet.")

What is it?

("An alkaloid, probably from some local root.")

What's it supposed to do to me?

("Put you out of the picture for the rest of the night.")

Dalt pondered this. *I wonder what for?*

("I haven't the faintest. But while they're all still distracted by Anthon's departure, I suggest you pour your wine out on the floor immediately. It will mix with Anthon's and no one will be the wiser. You may then proceed to amaze these yokels with your continuing consciousness.")

I have a better idea, Dalt thought as he poured the wine along the outside of his boot so that it would strike the floor in a smooth silent flow instead of a noisy splash. *I'll wait a few minutes and then pass out. Maybe that way we'll find out what they've got in mind.*

("Sounds risky.")

Nevertheless, that's what we'll do.

Dalt decided to make the most of the time he had left before passing out. "You know," he said, feigning a deep swallow of wine, "I saw a bright light streak across the sky last night. It fell to the earth far beyond the horizon. I've heard tales lately of such a light coming to rest in this region, some even say it landed on Bendelema itself. Is this true or merely the mutterings of vassals in their cups?"

The table chatter ceased abruptly. So did all eating and drinking. Every face at the table stared in Dalt's direction.

"Why do you ask this, Racso?" the Duke said. The curtain of suspicion which had seemed to vanish at the beginning of the meal had again been drawn closed between Racso and the Duke.

Dalt decided it was time for his exit. "My only interest, Your Lordship, is in the idle tales I've heard. I . . ." He half rose from his seat and put a hand across his eyes. "I . . ." Carefully, he allowed himself to slide to the floor.

"Carry him upstairs," said the Duke.

"Why don't we put an end to his meddling now, Your Lordship," suggested one of the advisers.

"Because he's a friend of Anthon's and he may well mean us no harm. We will know tomorrow."

With little delicacy and even less regard for his physical well-being, Dalt was carried up to his room and unceremoniously dumped on the bed. The heavy sound of the hardwood door slamming shut was followed by the click of a key in the lock.

Dalt sprang up and checked the door. The key had been taken from the inside and left in the lock after being turned.

("So much for that bright idea,") Pard commented caustically.

"None of your remarks, if you please."

("What do we do, now that we're confined to quarters for the rest of the night?")

"What else?" Dalt said. He kicked off his boots, removed breastplate, jerkin, and breeches, and hopped into bed.

The door was unlocked the next morning and Dalt made his way downstairs as unobtrusively as possible. Strench's cell-like quarters were just off the kitchen, if memory served . . . yes, there it was. And Strench was nowhere about.

("What do you think you're doing?")

I'm doing my best to make sure we don't get stuck up there in that room again tonight. His gaze came to rest on the large board where Strench kept all the duplicate keys for the locks of the keep.

("I begin to understand.")

Slow this morning, aren't you?

Dalt took the duplicate key to his room off its hook and replaced it with another, similar key from another part of the board. Strench might realize at some time during the day that a key was missing, but he'd be looking for the wrong one.

Dalt ran into the majordomo moments later.

"His Lordship wishes to see you, Racso," he said stiffly.

"Where is he?"

"On the North Wall."

("This could be a critical moment.")

"Why do you say that, Pard?" Dalt muttered.

("Remember last night, after you pulled your dramatic collapsing act? The Duke said something about finding out about you today.")

"And you think this could be it?"

("Could be. I'm not sure, of course, but I'm glad you have that dagger in your belt.")

The Duke was alone on the wall and greeted Dalt/Racso as warmly as his aloof manner would permit after the latter apologized for "drinking too much" the night before.

"I'm afraid I have a small confession to make," the Duke said.

"Yes, Your Lordship?"

"I suspected you of treachery when you first arrived." He held up a gloved hand as Dalt opened his mouth to reply. "Don't protest your innocence. I've just heard from a spy in the Tependian court and he says you have not set foot in Tependia since your mysterious disappearance years ago."

Dalt hung his head. "I am grieved, M'Lord."

"Can you blame me, Racso? Everyone knows that you hire out to the highest bidder, and Tependia has taken an inordinate interest in what goes on in Bendelema lately, even to the extent of sending raiding parties into our territory to carry off some of my vassals."

"Why would they want to do that?"

The Duke puffed up with pride. "Because Bendelema has become a land of plenty. As you know, that last harvest was plentiful everywhere; and, as usual, the present crop is stunted every-where . . . except in Bendelema." Dalt didn't know that but he nodded anyway. So only Bendelema was having a second bumper crop—that was interesting.

"I suppose you have learned some new farming methods and Tependia wants to steal them," Dalt suggested.

"That and more." The Duke nodded. "We also have new storage methods and new planting methods. When the next famine comes, we shall overcome Tependia not with swords and firebrands, but with food! The starving Tependians will leave their lord and Bendelema will extend its boundaries!"

Dalt was tempted to say that if the Tependians were snatching up vassals and stealing Bendelema's secrets, there just might not be another famine. But the Duke was dreaming of empire and it is not always wise for a mere mercenary to interrupt a duke's dreams of empire. Dalt remained silent as the Duke stared at the horizon he soon hoped to own.

The rest of the day was spent in idle search of rumors and by the dinner hour Dalt was sure of one thing: The ship had crashed or landed in the clearing he had inspected a few days before. More than that was known, but the Bendeleman locals were keeping it to themselves—*yes, I saw the light come down; no, I saw nothing else.*

Anthon again offered him the head table and Dalt accepted. When the Duke was toasted, Dalt took only a tiny sip.

What's the verdict, Pard?

("Same as last night.")

*I wonder what this is all about. They don't drug
me at lunch or breakfast—why only at dinner?*

("Tonight we'll try to find out.")

Since there was no outburst from Anthon this
time, Dalt was hard put to find a way to get rid of
his drugged wine. He finally decided to feign a
collapse again and spill his cup in the process,
hoping to hide the fact that he had taken only a
few drops.

After slumping forward on the table, he listened
intently.

"How long is this to go on, Father? How can we
drug him every night without arousing his suspicions?" It was Anthon's voice.

"As long as you insist on quartering him here
instead of with the other men-at-arms!" the Duke
replied angrily. "We cannot have him wandering
about during the nightly services. He's an outsider
and must not learn of the godling!"

Anthon's voice was sulky. "Very well . . . I'll
have him move out to the barracks tomorrow."

"I'm sorry, Anthon," the Duke said in a milder
tone. "I know he's a friend of yours, but the godling must come before a mercenary."

("I have a pretty good idea of the nature of this
godling,") Pard said as Dalt/Racso was carried
upstairs.

*The brain? I was thinking that, too. But how
would the brain communicate with these people?
The proto-type wasn't set up for it.*

("Why do you drag in communication? Isn't it
enough that it came from heaven?")

*No. The brain doesn't look godlike in the least.
It would have to communicate with the locals be-*

fore they'd deify it. Otherwise, the crash of the ship would be just another fireside tale for the children.

In a rerun of the previous night's events, Dalt was dumped on his bed and the door was locked from the outside. He waited a few long minutes until everything was silent beyond the door, then he poked the duplicate key into the lock. The original was pushed out on the other side and landed on the stone floor with a night-marishly loud *clang*. But no other sounds followed, so Dalt twisted his own key and slinked down the hall to the stairway that overlooked the dining area.

Empty. The plates hadn't even been cleared away.

"Now where'd everybody go?" Dalt muttered.

("Quiet! Hear those voices?")

Dalt moved down the stairs, listening. A muted chanting seemed to fill the chamber. A narrow door stood open to his left and the chanting grew louder as he approached it.

This is it . . . they must have gone through here.

The passage within, hewn from earth and rock, led downward and Dalt followed it. Widely spaced torches sputtered flickering light against the rough walls and the chanting grew louder as he moved.

Can you make out what they're saying?

("Something about the sacred objects, half of which must be placed in communion with the sun one day and the other half placed in communion with the sun the next day . . . a continuous cycle.")

The chant suddenly ended.

("It appears the litany is over. We had better go back.")

No, we're hiding right here. The brain is no doubt in there and I want to get back to civilization as soon as possible.

Dalt crouched in a shadowed sulcus in the wall and watched as the procession passed, the Duke in the lead, carrying some cloth-covered objects held out before him, Anthon sullenly following. The court advisers plucked the torches from the walls as they moved, but Dalt noticed that light still bled from the unexplored end of the passage. He sidled along the wall toward it after the others had passed.

He was totally unprepared for the sight that greeted his eyes as he entered the terminal alcove.

It was surreal. The vaulted subterranean chamber was strewn with the wreckage of the lost cargo ship. Huge pieces of twisted metal lay stacked against the walls; small pieces hung suspended from the ceiling. And foremost and center, nearly indistinguishable from the other junk, sat the silvery life-support apparatus of the brain, as high as a man and twice as broad.

And atop that—the brain, a ball of neural tissue floating in a nutrient bath within a crystalline globe.

("You can't hear him, can you?") Pard said.

"Him? Him who?"

("The brain—it pictures itself as a him—did manage to communicate with the locals. You were right about that.")

"What are you talking about?"

("It's telepathic, Steve, and my presence in your brain seems to have blocked your reception. I sensed a few impulses back in the passage but I wasn't sure until it greeted us.")

"What's it saying?"

("The obvious: It wants to know who we are and what we want.") There was a short pause. ("Oh, oh! I just told it that we're here to take it back to SW and it let out a telepathic emergency call—a loud one. Don't be surprised if we have company in a few minutes.")

"Great! Now what do we do?" Dalt fingered the dagger in his belt as he pondered the situation. It was already too late to run and he didn't want to have to blast his way out. His eyes rested on the globe.

"Correct me if I'm wrong, Pard, but I seem to remember something about the globe being removable."

("Yes, it can be separated from the life-support system for about two hours with no serious harm to the brain.")

"That's just about all we'd need to get it back to the mothership and hooked up to another unit."

("He's quite afraid, Steve,") Pard said as Dalt began to disconnect the globe. ("By the way, I've figured out that little litany we just heard: The sacred objects that are daily put in 'communion with the sun' are solar batteries. Half are charged one day, half the next. That's how he keeps himself going.")

Dalt had just finished stoppering the globe's exchange ports when the Duke and his retinue arrived in a noisy, disorganized clatter.

"Racso!" The Duke cried on sight of him. "So you've betrayed us after all!"

"I'm sorry," Dalt said, "but this belongs to someone else."

Anthon lunged to the front. "Treacherous scum!
And I called you friend!" As the youth's hand
reached for his sword hilt, Dalt raised the globe.

"Stay your hand, Anthon! If any of you try to
bar my way, I'll smash this globe and your godling
with it!" The Duke blanched and laid a restraining
hand on his son's shoulder. "I didn't come here
with the idea of stealing something from you, but
steal it I must. I regret the necessity." Dalt wasn't
lying. He felt, justifiably, that he had betrayed a
trust and it didn't sit well with him, but he kept
reminding himself that the brain belonged to SW
and he was only returning it to them.

("I hope your threat holds them,") Pard said.
("If they consider the possibilities, they'll realize
that if they jump you, they'll lose their godling;
but if they let you go, they lose it anyway.")

At the moment Anthon voiced this same conclusion, but his father restrained him. "Let him take
the godling, my son. It has aided us with its wisdom, the least we can do is guarantee it safe
passage."

Dalt grabbed one of the retainers. "You run
ahead and ready me a horse—a good one!" He
watched him go, then slowly followed the passage
back to the dining area. The Duke and his group
remained behind in the alcove.

"I wonder what kind of plot they're hatching
against me now," Dalt whispered. "Imagine! All
the time I spent here never guessing they were
telepaths!"

("They're not, Steve.")

"Then how do they communicate with this thing?" he said, glancing at the globe under his arm.

("The brain is an exceptionally strong sender and receiver, that's the secret. These folk are no more telepathic than anyone else.")

Dalt was relieved to find the horse waiting and the gate open. The larger of Kwashi's two moons was well above the horizon and Dalt took the most direct route to his hidden shuttlecraft.

("Just a minute, Steve,") Pard said as Dalt dismounted near the ship's hiding place. ("We seem to have a moral dilemma on our hands.")

"What's that?" Pard had been silent during the entire trip.

("I've been talking to the brain and I think it's become a little more than just a piloting device.")

"Possibly. It crashed, discovered it was telepathic, and tried to make the best of the situation. We're returning it. What's the dilemma?"

("It didn't crash. It sounded the alarm to get rid of the technician and brought the ship down on purpose. And it doesn't want to go back.")

"Well, it hasn't got much choice in the matter. It was made by SW and that's where it's going."

("Steve, it's *pleading* with us!")

"Pleading?"

("Yes. Look, you're still thinking of this thing as a bunch of neurons put together to pilot a ship, but it's developed into something more than that. It's now a *being*, and a thinking, reasoning, volitional one at that! It's no longer a biomechanism, it's an intelligent creature!")

"So you're a philosopher now, is that it?"

("Tell me, Steve. What's Barre going to do when he gets his hands on it?")

Dalt didn't want to answer that one.

("He's no doubt going to dissect it, isn't he?")

"He might not . . . not after he learns it's intelligent."

("Then let's suppose Barre doesn't dissect him—I mean *it* . . . no, I mean *him*. Never mind. If Barre allows it to live, the rest of its life will be spent as an experimental subject. Is that right? Are we justified in delivering it up for that?")

Dalt didn't answer.

("It's not causing any harm. As a matter of fact, it may well help put Kwashi on a quicker road back to civilization. It wants no power. It memorized the ship's library before it crashed and it was extremely happy down there in the alcove, doling out information about fertilizers and crop rotation and so forth and having its batteries charged every day.")

"I'm touched," Dalt muttered sarcastically.

("Joke if you will, but I don't take this lightly.")

"Do you have to be so self-righteous?"

("I'll say no more. You can leave the globe here and the brain will be able to telepathically contact the keep and they'll come out and get it.")

"And what do I tell Clarkson?"

("Simply tell him the truth, up to the final act, and then say that the globe was smashed at the keep when they tried to jump you and you barely escaped with your life.")

"That may kill the brain project, you know. Retrieval of the brain is vital to its continuance."

("That may be so, but it's a risk we'll have to

take. If, however, your report states that the brain we were after had developed a consciousness and self-preservation tendencies, a lot of academic interest will surely be generated and research will go on, one way or the other.")

Much to his dismay, Dalt found himself agreeing with Pard, teetering on the brink of gently placing the globe in the grass and walking away, saying to hell with SW.

("It's still pleading with us, Steve. Like a child.")

"All right, dammit!"

Cursing himself for a sucker and a softy, Dalt walked a safe distance from the shuttlecraft and put down the globe.

"But there's a few things we've got to do before we leave here."

("Like What?")

"Like filling in our little friend here on some of the basics of feudal culture, something that I'm sure was not contained in his ship's library."

("He'll learn from experience.")

"That's what I'm afraid of. Without a clear understanding of Kwashi's feudalism, his aid to Bendelema might well unbalance the whole social structure. An overly prosperous duchy is either overcome by jealous, greedy neighbors, or it uses its prosperity to build an army and pursue a plan of conquest. Either course could prove fatal to the brain and further hinder Kwashi's chances for social and technological rehabilitation."

("So what's your plan?")

"A simple one: You'll take all I know about Kwashi and feudalism and feed it to the brain. And you can stress the necessity of finding a means for wider dissemination of its knowledge, such as telepathically dropping bits of information into the heads of passing merchants, minstrels, and vagabonds. If this prosperity can be spread out over a wide area, there'll be less chance of social upheaval. All of Kwashi will benefit in the long run."

Pard complied and began the feeding process. The brain had a voracious appetite for information and the process was soon completed. As Dalt rose to his feet, he heard a rustling in the bushes. Looking up, he saw Anthon striding toward him with a bared sword.

"I've decided to return the godling," Dalt stammered lamely.

Anthon stopped. "I don't want the filthy thing! As a matter of fact, I intend to smash it as soon as I finish with you!" There was a look of incredible hatred in his eyes, the look of a young man who has discovered that his friend and admired instructor is a treacherous thief.

"But the godling has seen to it that no one in Bendelema will ever again go hungry!" Dalt said. "Why destroy it?"

"Because it has also seen to it that no one in the court of Bendelema will ever look up to me as Duke!"

"They look up to your father. Why not you in your turn?"

"They look up to my father out of habit!" he snarled. "But it is the godling who is the source of authority in Bendelema! And when my father is gone, I shall be nothing but a puppet."

Dalt now understood Anthon's moodiness: The brain threatened his position.

"So you followed me not in spite of my threat to smash the godling but because of it!"

Anthon nodded and began advancing again. "I also had a score to settle with you, Racso! I couldn't allow you to betray my trust and the trust of my father and go *unpunished!*" With the last word he aimed a vicious chop at Dalt, who ducked, spun, and dodged out of the way. He had not been wearing his sword when he left his room back at the keep, and consequently did not have it with him now. But he had the dagger.

Anthon laughed at the sight of the tiny blade. "Think you can stop me with that?"

If you only knew! Dalt thought. He didn't want to use the blaster, however. He understood Anthon's feelings. If there were only some way he could stun him and make his escape.

Anthon attacked ferociously now and Dalt was forced to back-peddle. His foot caught on a stone and as he fell he instinctively threw his free hand out for balance. The ensuing events seemed to occur in slow motion. He felt a jarring, crushing, cutting, agonizing pain in his left wrist and saw Anthon's blade bite through it. The hand flew off as if with a life of its own, and a pulsing stream of red shot into the air. Dalt's right hand, too, seemed to take on a life of its own as it reversed the dagger, pointed the butt of the hilt at Anthon, and pressed the hidden stud. An energy bolt, blinding in the darkness, struck him in the chest and he went down without a sound.

Dalt grabbed his forearm. "My hand!" he screamed in agony and horror.

("Give me control!") Pard said urgently.

"My hand!" was all Dalt could say.

(*"Give me control!"*)

Dalt was jolted by this. He relaxed for a second and suddenly found himself an observer in his own body. His right hand dropped the dagger and cupped itself firmly over the bleeding stump, the thumb and fingers digging into the flesh of his forearm, searching for pressure points on the arteries.

His legs straightened as he rose to his feet and calmly walked toward the concealed shuttlecraft. His elbows parted the bushes and jabbed the plate that operated the door to the outer lock.

("I'm glad you didn't lock this up yesterday,") Pard said as the port swung open. There was a first-aid emergency kit inside for situations such as this. The pinky of his right hand was spared from its pressure duty to flip open the lid of the kit and then a container of stat-gel. The right hand suddenly released its grasp and, amid a splatter of blood, the stump of his left arm was forcefully shoved into the gel and held there.

("That should stop the bleeding.") The gel had an immediate clotting effect on any blood that came into contact with it. The thrombus formed would be firm and tough.

Rising, Dalt discovered that his body was his own again. He stumbled outside, weak and disoriented.

"You saved my life, Pard," he mumbled finally. "When I looked at that stump with the blood shooting out, I couldn't move."

("I saved *our* life, Steve.")

He walked over to where Anthon lay with a

smoking hole where his chest had been. "I wished to avoid that. It wasn't really fair, you know. He only had a sword. . . ." Dalt was not quite himself yet. The events of the last minute had not yet been absorbed.

("Fair, hell! What does 'fair' mean when someone's trying to kill you?")

But Dalt didn't seem to hear. He began searching the ground. "My hand! Where's my hand? If we bring it back maybe they can replace it!"

("Not a chance, Steve. Necrosis will be in full swing by the time we get to the mothership.")

Dalt sat down. The situation was finally sinking in. "Oh, well," he said resignedly. "They're doing wonderful things with prosthetics these days."

("Prosthetics! We'll grow a *new* one!")

Dalt paused before answering. "A new hand?"

("Of course! You've still got deposits of omnipotential mesenchymal cells here and there in your body. I'll just have them transported to the stump, and with me guiding the process there'll be no problem to rebuilding the hand. It's really too bad you humans have no conscious control over the physiology of your bodies. With the proper direction, the human body is capable of almost anything.")

"You mean I'll have my hand back? Good as new?"

("Good as new. But at the moment I suggest we get into the ship and depart. The brain has called the Duke and it might be a good thing if we weren't here when he arrived.")

"You know," Dalt said as he entered the shuttlecraft and let the port swing to a close behind him, "with you watching over my body, I could live to a ripe old age."

("All I have to do is keep up with the degenerative changes and you'll live forever.")

Dalt stopped in midstride. "Forever?"

("Of course. The old natives of this planet knew it when they made up that warning for their children: 'Of every thousand struck down, nine hundred and ninety-nine will die.' The obvious conclusion is that the thousandth victim will *not* die.")

"Ever?"

("Well, there's not much I can do if you catch an energy bolt in the chest like Anthon back there. But otherwise, you won't die of old age—I'll see to that. You won't even get old, for that matter.")

The immensity of what Pard was saying suddenly struck Dalt with full force. "In other words," he breathed, "I'm immortal."

("I'd prefer a different pronoun: *We* are immortal.")

"I don't believe it."

("I don't care what you believe. I'm going to keep you alive for a long, long time, Steve, because while *you* live, *I* live, and I've grown very fond of living.")

Dalt did not move, did not reply.

("Well, what are you waiting for? There's a whole galaxy of worlds out there just waiting to be seen and experienced and I'm getting damn sick of this one!")

Dalt smiled. "What's the hurry?"

There was a pause, then: ("You've got a point there, Steve. There's really no hurry at all. We've got all the time in the world. Literally.")

The further adventures of
Steven Dalt (and Pard)
will continue in

HEALER

coming soon from

BAEN BOOKS

FRED SABERHAGEN

Fred Saberhagen needs very little introduction these days. His most famous creations—the awesome Berserkers—are known to SF readers around the world. He's reached the bestseller lists several times, most recently with his "Book of Swords" series, and his novels span the territory from hard science fiction to high fantasy. Quite understandably, Saberhagen's been labeled one of the best writers in the business.

These fine novels by Saberhagen are available from Baen Books:

PYRAMIDS

A fascinating new twist on the time-travel novel, introducing a great new series hero: Pilgrim, the Flying Dutchman of Time, whose only hope for returning home lies in subtly altering the history of our own timeline to more closely reflect his own. Fortunately for us, Pilgrim's timeline is a rather more pleasant one than ours, and so the changes are—or at least are supposed to be—for the better. Learn why the curse of the Pharaoh Khufu (builder of the Great Pyramid) had a special reality, in *Pyramids*. "Saberhagen's light, imaginative and enjoyable adventures speed along twisting paths to a climax that is even more surprising than the rest of the book."
—*Publishers Weekly*

AFTER THE FACT

This is the second novel featuring the great new series hero, Pilgrim—the Lost Traveller adrift in time and dimensionality. His current project: to rescue Abraham Lincoln from assassination, AFTER THE FACT!

THE FRANKENSTEIN PAPERS
At last—the truth about the sinister Dr. Frankenstein and his monster with a heart of gold, based on a history written by the monster himself! Find out what happened when the mad Doctor brought his creation to life, and why the monster has no scars.

THE "EMPIRE OF THE EAST" SERIES
THE BROKEN LANDS, Book I
A masterful blend of high technology and high sorcery; a unique adventure in a world on the brink of ultimate change; a world were magic rules—and science struggles to live again! "*Empire of the East* is one of the best science fiction fantasy epics—Saberhagen can be justly proud. Highly recommended."—*Science Fiction Review*. "A fine mix of fantasy and science fiction, action and speculation."—Roger Zelazny

THE BLACK MOUNTAINS, Book II
East meets West in bloody conflict on a world where magic rules, but technology is revolting! "*Empire of the East* is the work of a master!"—*Magazine of Fantasy and Science Fiction*

ARDNEH'S WORLD, Book III
The gripping climax of the "Empire of the East" series. "Ranks favorably with Tolkien. Exceptional in sheer unbridled zest and imaginative sweep."—*School Library Journal*

* * *

THE GOLDEN PEOPLE
Genetically perfect, super-human children are created by a dedicated scientist for the betterment of Mankind. As the children mature, however, they begin to wonder if Man *should* survive . . .

LOVE CONQUERS ALL
In a future where childbirth is outlawed and promiscuity required, one woman dares fight the system for the right to bear children.

MY BEST
Saberhagen presents his personal best, in *My Best*. One sure to please lovers of "hard" science fiction as well as high fantasy.

OCTAGON
Players scattered across the continent are engaged in a game called "Starweb." Each player has certain attributes, and can ally with or attack any of the others. But one player seems to have confused the reality of the world: a player with the attributes of machinelike precision and mechanical ruthlessness. His name is Octagon, and he's out for blood.

You can order all of Fred Saberhagen's books with this order form. Check your choices and send the combined cover price/s to: Baen Books, Dept. BA, 260 Fifth Avenue, New York, New York 10001.

PYRAMIDS • 320 pp. •
65609-0 • $3.50   _____

AFTER THE FACT • 320 pp. •
65391-1 • $3.95   _____

THE FRANKENSTEIN PAPERS •
288 pp. • 65550-7 $3.50   _____

THE BROKEN LANDS • 224 pp. •
65380-6 • $2.95   _____

THE BLACK MOUNTAINS • 192 pp.
• 65390-3 • $2.75   _____

ARDNEH'S WORLD, Book III •
192 pp. • 65404-7 • $2.75   _____

THE GOLDEN PEOPLE • 272 pp. •
55904-4 • $3.50   _____

LOVE CONQUERS ALL • 288 pp. •
55953-2 • $2.95   _____

MY BEST • 320 pp. • 65645-7 •
$2.95   _____

OCTAGON • 288 pp. •
65353-9 • $2.95   _____